SILVER GOODBYE

John H. Cunningham

Other books by John H. Cunningham

Red Right Return

Green to Go

Crystal Blue

Second Chance Gold

Maroon Rising

Free Fall to Black

SILVER GOODBYE

John H. Cunningham

SILVER GOODBYE

Copyright © 2018 John H. Cunningham

All rights reserved. No part of this book may be reproduced or retransmitted in any form or by any means without the written permission of the publisher.

Published by Greene Street, LLC

Print ISBN: 978-0-9987965-3-6
Electronic ISBN: 978-0-9987965-2-9

The events and characters in this book are fictitious. Certain real locations and public figures are mentioned, but have been used fictitiously, and all other characters and events in the book have been invented.

www.jhcunningham.com

This book is for
Pepe, Raquel, Santiago and Oliver Gonzalez

Good friends are
like stars.
you don't always
see them,
but you know they're
always there.

"The "Pepes" modus operandi includes bombings, assassinations, kidnappings and intimidation at the infrastructure of Pablo Escobar's organization." Counterdrug Division, Defense Intelligence Agency

"This (Irma) is a deadly storm and our state has never seen anything like it," Governor of Florida, Rick Scott said. "Once the storm starts, law enforcement cannot save you."

SECTION 1

IMMINENT DANGER

PROLOGUE

A ROOSTER CROWED BEHIND ME AND I NEARLY CHOKED on my double espresso. I was seated on a bench by Cuban Coffee Queen on Southard, a short walk from my suite at the La Concha hotel. Morning was my favorite time in Key West. The tourists were asleep, the drunks had passed out, business owners took their time getting started for the day, and chickens roamed freely on the sidewalks and streets. August was the most oppressive month here in the tropics, so early morning was the best time to avoid the shirt-soaking heat and humidity.

> MISSING PERSON: Searching for any information about Charlie Reilly who lived in Key West in the 80s and early 90s. Please email: info@keycitizen classified.ID.556.2017

Someone had left a newspaper on the bench and I paged through without reading anything but headlines. News from the outside world no longer interested me. The classified ads at the end were brief and often entertaining. I held the paper closer.

The hand holding the paper shook. My given name, Charles B. Reilly III, was pretty rare, but drop the *B* and the *III* and it was pretty common. I had dropped it all and gone by Buck after my company, e-Antiquity, went bankrupt several years ago. Awfully coincidental that someone named Charlie Reilly lived in Key West in the '80s and '90s and, according to this ad, had gone missing. And why the hell would someone run an ad for a missing person nearly thirty years later?

When the rooster crowed from under my bench, I flinched and swatted the paper at him before watching him strut off.

1

THREE WEEKS LATER

EVERYTHING THAT WAS LEFT OF MY PARENTS, who'd been killed in Switzerland nearly ten years ago, was laid out before me in neat piles. Their ashes in matching urns, photographs, mementos, files, journals with the dank smell of decay from being left in a trunk all that time.

I sat inside the barn of what had once been their farm in Middleburg, Virginia, on the mounting block my mother had used to climb aboard her horses. The wood walls of the tack room were covered with photographs of long-dead horses, their frames now so coated with dust it looked like a fungus. Cobwebs hung from the ceiling, and the air was stale from the room's being locked tight since my last visit just after they were killed.

I didn't want to be here now, but my brother had asked me to housesit for him while he was off in the South of France with his latest girlfriend. We weren't close. The fact that the tanking of e-Antiquity and our parents' deaths had happened simultaneously had led the FBI and Interpol to try to hold me responsible for their deaths, which fractured Ben's and my relationship beyond repair. That's why his call for help had felt like an opportunity.

A shiver sat me up straight and I again looked at the piles on the floor. Hard to believe these few items were all that remained from lives as remarkable as my parents'. With a long and decorated career at the State Department, two presidents had considered my father as a candidate for secretary of state. His reputation as a no-nonsense maverick had ultimately scared them off, presidents generally preferring yes-men. Mom had been a tireless scion of the community, chairwoman on many a non-profit board. A decorated equestrian, she was the epitome of horse-country class here in Middleburg, where they'd settled in their thirties not long after I was born.

A snapshot of my family taken after a day of snorkeling and boating several miles off the coast of Key West on what we referred to as Shark Beach stared up at me from the top of the picture pile. Just kids then, Ben and I were laughing, but my mother's lips were pressed tight. Her anger at my father for letting us swim with sharks had been forever captured on film.

I smiled. "It's okay, Mom. We survived."

The echo of my voice in the otherwise empty room wiped the smile clean. I turned to a file labeled "Charles B. Reilly III" that, along with Dad's journals, had been locked in the bottom drawer of his desk in the house. I had a pretty good idea what it contained but had never opened it.

I tore the yellowed envelope open. The stationery heading, "Washington DC Adoption Bureau," proved me right. These were my adoption papers.

The three-page document had many of the same elements as a bill of sale. It was dated a few days after my birth date and had my birth specs: twenty-one inches long and eight pounds, four ounces. Hair blond, eyes blue. Healthy. The next page had my parents' names, their home address at the time, in northwest Washington, D.C., and some legalese about agreeing to care for me.

All as expected, except for the last page. It was an affidavit from the British Embassy waiving rights to my citizenship—I was born British?

What the hell?

There was no birth certificate, no names identifying my birth parents. There was a serial number for my case, as I'm sure there were with all adoptions, and that was it.

Strange.

I folded up the papers and placed them back in the envelope.

I refocused on my father's journals. Seeing his handwriting sent a warm sensation through me. There were three black books and one spiral-bound brown notebook. The first black book contained names, dates, and locations of meetings my father had attended on State Department business. Every page was full. The names that jumped out at me were Hamid Karzai, Wen Jiabao, Moshe Katsav, Jacques Chirac, Vladimir Putin, and Fidel Castro.

Wow.

He really could have been secretary of state.

The other black books were similarly filled with names of heads of state, foreign ministers, and diplomats along with the dates of their meetings. Most I didn't recognize, but given the locations and chronological order, I realized just how much Dad had traveled on behalf of the country. Maybe someday I'd put pins on a map of all the places he'd been and number them to show the order. Would his meetings coincide with major negotiations of the times? Successes and failures?

The oldest of the four journals was on the bottom of the pile. It was a brown spiral-bound notebook that was totally different from its black brothers.

The handwriting was much looser, hurried, there was far less order, and some of the sentences made no sense. There were city names and dates going back to the late 1980s and early 1990s. I fanned through the pages and realized there was a much tighter pattern of locations than in his black journals. In the brown one he'd noted trips to Bogota, Cartagena, Cali, Panama, Havana, Medellín, Miami.

And Key West.

My father's career in the State Department didn't start until the late nineties. What was he doing in Colombia, Panama, Cuba, and South Florida in the late eighties and early nineties?

2

THE AIR WAS THICK OUTSIDE THE BARN, this August was right up there with the worst ones I remembered from my youth. I missed the ocean breeze that offset the heat in the Keys.

So much for catching a breath of fresh air.

The afternoon light was on the wane, and a thin line of pink and purple had begun to form along the Blue Ridge Mountains on the horizon. But my mind was still focused on the contents of my father's old brown notebook. There were fifty pages of cryptic notes, many of which were dates and names, most of which were Hispanic, usually just a first or last name.

The muggy air drove me back inside. Ben would be home in a couple of days and I planned to leave for Key West the moment he arrived. Hurricane Harvey had just decimated coastal Texas, and I was relieved it had missed the Keys. No way to reason with hurricane season when you live on an island in the tropics.

Again seated on the mounting block, I reopened the brown notebook. At the end was half of a crude map. The other half had been torn out. The last entry in the book was dated October 1992, from Key West. Two names were listed—Tommy Diaz and Frank Graves—along with some numbers:

17000 / 50 # 12000 / 100 # 10,000 / 20 ### LO / SP / EP / ES

Perspiration clung to my shirt in the non-air conditioned room. I packed the four journals, my adoption papers, and the handful of old pictures with the photo from Shark Beach on top into a box. I replaced the padlock on the door and hustled my way through the humidity back to the main house, where the air-conditioning was on high and a half bottle of Pilar dark rum awaited.

Ben had redecorated much of the house using some of the money inherited from our parents. They'd left me nothing, because according to Carlton Grooms, our family attorney, my net worth had been north of twenty million dollars when the wills were codified. I'd had a few successes since then, so I no longer needed the monthly stipend Ben had initially provided me after my bankruptcy.

I poured three fingers of Pilar into a Waterford glass and dropped a few ice cubes in. A photo of Ben and his girlfriend, Julie, an heiress from a candy dynasty who lived nearby, caught my eye. She was somewhat plain for my taste, but Ben had told me there were billions of reasons for him to love her. I've never seen a cash cow produce anything but sour milk, but I'd wished him luck.

I sat at the kitchen table where Ben had left his computer, took a sip of the smooth rum, and retrieved the brown notebook from the box. The Weather Channel blared from the TV on the counter.

"Hurricane Harvey has made landfall in Louisiana five days after first hitting Texas. This historic storm has caused more damage than any other in history…"

That damn hurricane had ricocheted around the northern Gulf of Mexico like the Tasmanian Devil for a week solid. The fact that it had now made landfall again was incredibly bad luck.

Back to the brown notebook with its many names, most of them cited in Colombia in the eighties and nineties. An uneasy sensation caused me to take a gulp of rum. The last time I saw my father was when I gave him the maps and clues to other potential treasures I had spirited away from e-Antiquity. As it turned out, this had been the night before the FBI and the SEC closed us down. Initially shocked at what was happening, my father's last words surprised and confused me then but now had me as curious as I could recall ever being in my life.

"I wasn't always a Boy Scout, Buck."

Would the brown notebook provide insight into that ... comment? Confession?

I settled on a page in the middle. Two names appeared with several dates: Carlos Castaño and Fidel Castaño. After a quick Google search I learned that they were the founders and leaders of the Colombian National Army, a murderous paramilitary force that had once provided muscle for Pablo Escobar's Medellín cartel, only to turn on them later. They had another brother, Vincente, and according to the article I'd found, Vincente had killed Carlos for control of their private army.

Had my father known them?

Apparently so, given how often their names appeared throughout the notebook. But why?

It suddenly hit me that I knew very little about my father's life before the State Department. He'd worked there for as long as I'd lived, but by his own admission he wasn't always a Boy Scout.

I found another name, Jose Gonzalo Diaz Gacha, listed several times, then an *X* next to the last mention of his name with the date December 15, 1989. Thirty seconds on the Internet explained why. Gonzalo, a key member of the Medellín cartel, had been murdered on December 15, 1989.

I stared at the screen, then again at the notebook. Why had my father recorded the day a drug smuggler had been murdered?

I searched more names. All had been murdered.

According to multiple articles online, all their deaths were attributed to a vigilante group known as Los Pepes: People Persecuted by Pablo Escobar—in Spanish, *Perseguidos por Pablo Escobar*.

Los Pepes.

What the hell?

3

THE NAMES OF DEAD MEN in my father's journals had me digging through the box of material I'd brought inside the house. In the stack of photos was the one of the family at Shark Beach, followed by several others from my childhood. I shuffled them like playing cards until I found a few near the bottom. The first one caused my jaw to drop open.

It was of my father, in his twenties, wearing shorts and no shirt—holding a Thompson submachine gun in one hand and a .357 Magnum revolver in the other.

Both weapons were extended and pointed to the side. I couldn't see what he was aiming at. Palm trees were in the background, but there was no other indication of the location. Nothing was written on the backs of the photos, and there was no date stamped on them. I stared at the image of him with the guns for a long time.

Dad with a machine gun?

Los Pepes?

"What the hell?"

Another old photo was of Dad and two other guys his age. Their hair was parted down the middle and feathered back, they had moustaches, and they wore jeans and open-collared silk shirts that showed off gold chains around their necks. I guessed the photos to be from the late eighties or early nineties. That would be around the same time that Pablo Escobar's reign of violence had been at its height and just before Los Pepes began killing Medellín Cartel members.

Also inside the brown notebook was the hand-drawn map that had been torn in half. I studied the crude map, which included a note about "future furniture" and what looked like a depiction of the edge of three buildings. There was an arrow in the middle and a long oval shape on the top that bled off the torn part of the page.

I'd made (and lost) a fortune searching for and finding lost treasures, some a thousand years old. But success had always come through cross-referencing small disparate details until connections could be established and a trail could be followed. But this map provided nothing I could use.

"Tropical Depression Irma is building to what could be another massive hurricane and is now accelerating west of the Cape Verde Islands," said the pretty anchorwoman on the Weather Channel. "Computer models show the storm heading west through the Caribbean and into South Florida."

"Such bullshit," I said.

Every storm had a name and an advertising campaign these days. Paranoia promotion was no better than yelling "fire" in a crowded movie theater. Irma had thousands of miles to travel before it was anywhere near the Caribbean. How could models predict anything from that distance?

I dug through the box I'd brought in from the barn. There was an address book with scattered entries. Aside from my grandparents', there were only a few names, none of which I recognized. Three had out-of-country exchanges, 011-57, and two had 305 area codes and the prefixes 296 and 294. Those I recognized. Key West, Florida.

The Key West numbers belonged to Frank Graves and Tommy Diaz, who had been mentioned in the brown notebook. Could they be the two guys in the picture with Dad? I suddenly recalled the missing-person classified ad I'd seen in the *Citizen* a few weeks ago—could the ad's Charlie Reilly be my father? Had he actually lived there?

Many of the notes mentioned Colombia, but I'd never conducted an archaeological expedition there, so my knowledge of the country was limited. Worse, I had no contacts that could help me piece together the random details of Dad's notes and photos.

An idea struck me. Craig Dettra, a prominent archaeologist affiliated with the Smithsonian—and husband to my former lover and e-Antiquity research partner Scarlet Roberson—was a Colombian expert. Chances were Craig would know about other aspects of Colombian history, like Los Pepes.

Scarlet had been a researcher extraordinaire as well as a redheaded beauty I'd shared my travel tent with in many countries. Of course, I'd left Scarlet cold shortly after our biggest treasure-hunting success in Guatemala when I met supermodel Heather Drake, who for good reason became my future ex-wife. Would Scarlet still be bitter about that? Maybe she and Craig would be willing to help me shed some light on Colombia.

I found their number in Washington. Close by. A male voice answered when I dialed it.

"Craig, it's me, Buck Reilly. How are you?"

"Reilly? Damn, man, I haven't heard your voice—or name—in years."

Was he going to be an asshole? Best to make this quick.

"You were once considered an expert on Colombian history—"

"Still am. You have a project down there you need big-boy help with?"

"Ah, not really, just a mystery. Do you happen to know much about the seventies through nineties there, the drug trade, or the vigilante group known as Los Pepes?"

"Last Resort Charter now into flying drugs?"

"Charter *and* Salvage. No, it's a history project—nothing to do with lost treasure—"

He laughed, which felt like another dig. "Sounds fascinating. Wish I could help, but my area was pre-Colombian artifacts, not treasures hidden by dope smugglers."

"Of course." I paused. Would Scarlet help? Screw it. "How's Scarlet?"

"Touché, Reilly."

Huh? How had I scored a point in his game?

"I'm not following you," I said.

"I figured you knew. We're divorced. She and her boy live in Winter Park, Florida—have for a couple years."

Awkward. But my heart rate increased a beat.

"Sorry to hear that—"

"Spare me. You should call her—hang on, I'll even give you her number." I wrote it down.

"If you want help on something that happened a couple thousand years before the drug kingpins ruled Colombia, call me back."

"Thanks, Craig." I meant it.

The moment we disconnected, the house phone started to ring. I wouldn't have bothered to answer it except that, if it was Ben, I didn't want him to think I wasn't there. Would he know about any of this? Or would Carlton Grooms, Dad's attorney?

"Hello?"

"Buck, is that you?"

The harried voice of my aviation mechanic and friend—now business partner immediately registered.

"What's up, Ray? I thought I told you only to call this number in case of—"

"Emergency. That's why I'm calling."

"What's happened?" I placed my cell phone on the counter.

"There's another hurricane heading our way. People are freaking out."

"Tropical Depression Irma? It's a week away—"

"They're forecasting it will be a Category 2 storm by tomorrow."

"Come on, Ray. You're buying into the paranoia?"

"Doesn't matter if I'm buying into it or not. A lot of paying customers want to reserve charters with us to have their families and possessions evacuated before the storm hits the Keys."

"Seriously?"

"You *have* seen what Harvey did to Texas, haven't you?"

Not really. "Yes, but—"

"The European model projects the path—"

"How can any of that be accurate, Ray? The storm just left *Africa!*"

"Let me put it to you this way. Betty's about 75 percent restored and most of what's left is cosmetic, but that takes money you haven't got. You're not far from broke again."

"Thanks to your restoration estimate being grossly inaccurate."

"I had no idea how bad the previous renovation had been and couldn't have until I'd taken her apart." He sighed. "She's airworthy, so I could use her to fly people out of the Keys now, but her rough appearance could scare the crap out of cash-paying customers. So you need to get the Beauty home."

Ray and I had different opinions on the aesthetics and stability of the Beast, my 1946 Grumman Goose. It might be a beauty now, but she'd forever be the Beast in my mind, given what her condition had been when we repatriated her from Cuba.

"Ben will be back in a couple days. I'll leave then—"

"Five charter customers—and it's not even a hurricane yet. People are afraid South Florida will get swamped like Corpus Christie did, and we need the money."

I told Ray I'd be back as soon as I could and hung up.

Then I thought about Ben's Air France flight that would arrive the day after tomorrow and the long drive from Dulles airport, during which he would tell me all about the trip with his candy dynasty queen.

I glanced at the pile of journals, notes, and photographs—the one with Dad holding the guns now on top—and the address book with listings from Key West. Charter customers aside, what I'd pieced together from my father's past was reason enough for me to get home as soon as possible so I could start to research the information from the notebooks.

I wasn't always a Boy Scout, son.

"But could you have been a drug smuggler?"

4

BACK IN KEY WEST I FOUND THAT Ray was right. We had customers—mostly snowbirds who used their houses only during the winter months and now wanted to get their most precious possessions out of the Keys. Few Conchs, people born in the Keys who'd lived there all their lives, paid Irma much attention except for Pastor Willy Peebles from the Church of the Redeemer. Willy had asked—insistently—for me to take some elderly parishioners to safety.

I placed the packet of my father's mementos in the Beast's storage locker. Like so many other unsolved cases that filled my binder of old maps and clues to missing treasures, this one would have to wait. The next few days were filled with our gathering people's stuff from their homes, hauling it to the airport, and flying it up north, from Charlotte and Nashville to New York and Chicago. I called an old friend, Ron Weiner, to see if I could rent his empty airplane hangar at Spruce Creek Fly-in Community just west of Daytona Beach rather than make individual trips to each city. A generous soul, Ron agreed to let me use the hangar for free since it was related to storm evacuation.

The work was tedious and time-consuming. Ray and I used both planes to move eight families' loads to Ron's hangar over the course of four days. On the last trip, Ron greeted us with a bottle of Don Julio tequila. The television in the hangar was turned up loud. Ron was in his late seventies and in need of hearing aids, but he made up for not using them by talking at a deafening volume and cranking the television up as high as it would go.

"You boys are doing a hell of a service," he said. "Your customers are smart to clear out of the Keys."

"We've been so busy I haven't even checked on the storm," Ray said. "What's the latest?"

"Looky here. That foxy weather lady Anna Johnson will have you shaking in your flying boots."

He turned the volume up even louder.

"Tiny Barbuda, population one thousand, was literally wiped clean. Hurricane Irma is now a Category 5 storm with sustained winds of 135 mile per hour and is directly over the French West Indies—"

"Holy crap!" Ray said.

I nearly dropped the box of antique baby dolls that Willy Peebles's grandmother had wanted taken off-island.

"Wiped clean?" I said.

"You betcha," Ron said. "This storm is the real deal, boys. If she doesn't turn north soon, South Florida's in for a wallop."

The image on the large-screen TV showed Irma—over three hundred miles across—churning through the Caribbean like a Weedwacker through soft grass. My stomach flopped when I saw that the hurricane was directly over St. Barths. The butterfly-shaped island fit entirely inside the eye.

A Category 5 storm?

The French West Indies and the Caribbean would be mincemeat.

As the meteorologists had predicted, Hurricane Irma was a real threat—possibly not to the Keys, but my friends and many places I loved in the Caribbean were in serious peril.

Ray and I returned to Key West in separate planes. My mind was elsewhere, so radio conversation was minimal. The weather over the Keys was sunny, winds were light, and I was reminded that before mass communication and radar, deadly storms had appeared with virtually no warning other than a spiking barometer. The 1935 Labor Day hurricane had killed an estimated six hundred relief workers sent to the Keys to build roads at the height of the Great Depression.

They'd had no warning at all.

When the Beast was tied down and I had completed the post-flight checklist, I grabbed my backpack along with the packet of my father's journals and photos and locked the hatch.

"The airport is officially closed the day after tomorrow for the storm," Ray said. "I'll get the planes ready to go north to ride it out." My mind was elsewhere, but my head nodded.

I fired up my 1966 Land Rover Series II A 88, opened the windows, lifted the latches to allow fresh air to enter from below the wind screen, and lurched out of the parking lot. Instead of heading to Blue Heaven or back to the La Concha, I turned onto Atlantic Boulevard, then Ashby, and finally Rose Street and pulled up in front of a familiar brick rambler where four cars and a couple of old boats on trailers were parked out front.

The man I hoped to catch at home was sitting on the covered porch in a T-shirt and shorts, smoking a Parliament cigarette and sipping from a Michelob pony bottle. He was short and had a head full of gray hair parted down the middle. His skin was heavily wrinkled and tanned leather brown with age spots, and there were skin cancers on his forehead and cheeks. His eyes were sharp, though—made me think of an eagle perched on a branch watching a mouse meander just below him.

"What's up, cuz? Still driving that old jungle heap?"

"Hey, Currito. Wasn't sure if I'd find you here or at the jail."

"Shit, too many crackers from up north here as bondsmen now. My people are too old to be getting arrested, so I only get the random call now days."

Manuel "Currito" Salazar was a true Key West original. A native Conch now in his eighties, he'd lived through everything from the attempts to facilitate the Conch Republic's secession from the United States to purportedly being a smuggler back in the seventies and eighties.

"I'm guessing this isn't a social call," he said.

From the breast pocket of my fishing shirt I pulled out the pictures of my father. I handed them to Currito.

"Recognize any of these guys from the late eighties or early nineties?"

He placed them on the metal patio table next to him and dug a pair of smudged reading glasses from his pocket.

A high-pitched laugh lifted his head and he glanced quickly at me, then pulled the picture of my father and the two guys dressed nicely closer to his eyes.

"No shit, huh? Where the hell you find these?"

"You know 'em?"

"Know 'em? Yeah, I know 'em." He cackled with delight as he scrutinized each picture.

"So, who are they?"

"This one here"—Currito stabbed his finger at the face of one of the men—"was Tommy Diaz—"

"Was?"

"Got killed in Colombia by the Medellín cartel." His eyes focused on mine to gauge my response. I sat down suddenly on Currito's old ice chest.

He slid his finger to the right. "This one here is Frank Graves."

"He still alive?"

"Far as I know. Did twenty years in prison, for smuggling though. Been quiet ever since."

"He's here in Key West?"

"Floated around. Never got arrested again, though. I ain't seen him."

I waited, but I could tell Currito's mind was back a few decades remembering something, maybe the last time he saw these guys.

"What about that third guy?"

After another laugh, he lit a new cigarette and killed his beer. He shuffled the photos until he found the one of my father holding the Thompson submachine gun and the .357 Magnum.

"This one here's Crazy Charlie." Another cackle.

I licked my lips. "Was? He get killed in Colombia, too?"

"Not this one." He paused. The suspense had me edging forward on the cooler. "He disappeared, but I don't think he was killed. The cartel only did that to set examples and scare people. We'd of known."

"Why was he called Crazy Charlie?"

Currito laughed again. "Because he was freaking crazy. Fearless." He looked into my eyes again. I sensed he was searching for something. He took a drag from his cigarette. "Must have gone to Colombia twenty times."

I sat back. "I presume that wasn't as a tourist."

"Funny, kid."

A long silence dragged out. There was nothing funny about this quest—there was no question what kind of cartels Currito was referring to. Sweat beaded on my forehead.

"You look sick," he said. "Don't puke on my patio—"

"I'm fine."

"The hell's wrong with you?"

I leaned forward and studied his eyes.

"Buck?"

"Crazy Charlie …"

"Why you so interested in ancient history?"

"He was my father."

5

THE AFTERNOON PASSED IN A HAZE OF STORIES about my father that I would never have believed if they hadn't come from someone I trusted. Currito was a lot of things and could be accused of a lot more, but he was a straight shooter with his friends.

"Like I said, there was a lot of mystery around Charlie," he said, "both when he was running trips south and then after he disappeared."

"Didn't a lot of the smugglers get busted back then?"

"He was too smart. Guys who worked for him said Charlie's loads were never delivered to the same place twice. Hundreds of miles apart in several states." He smiled. "And no, they were never busted."

"If that's true, Charlie doesn't sound crazy to me," I said.

"Charlie was crazy-fearless. He smuggled more dope than anyone, no matter how much pressure the feds put on these islands. Everyone said so—again, people who knew firsthand."

"Other smugglers?"

"*Coño*, boy, you need a map?"

I picked up the picture of Dad, Diaz, and Graves.

"You said one of these guys got killed?"

"Tommy Diaz." He sighed. "He was your father's partner. When he got killed, your old man went into a rage."

"What happened?"

"Was in the early nineties. By then they'd been at it for a long time, more successful than most—"

"But how do you know?"

"Damn, cuz, because I was here. They were loaded—cash, cars, planes, boats, guns—like that one there." He pointed toward the picture of Dad holding the Thompson. "Charlie had crates of those things."

"Unbelievable."

"Anyway, Tommy's role was to coordinate directly with Medellín. Pablo Escobar himself. Word is they got sideways when the cartel started to implode—Escobar accused Tommy of double-dealing him. Then a couple of the senior guys got busted, some extradited, and when Escobar escaped from his own private prison, the shit hit the fan with Colombian government. Police turned up the heat and Escobar responded by killing hundreds if not thousands in Medellín and Bogota. Assassins and car bombs were his specialty. He even blew up a commercial passenger plane."

"I've seen *Narcos*."

"That's G-rated in comparison, believe me."

"So Tommy Diaz got blown up?"

"No, he was murdered by one of Escobar's men."

"After all that time and success. Why?"

"Nobody knew. Paranoia, loose ends, eliminating threats, could have been anything. But when pictures of Tommy dead were sent to your old man, he went ape shit. In fact, come to think of it, that's where the Crazy nickname came from."

I swallowed. "What'd he do?"

"Vowed revenge against the Medellín cartel."

Currito lit another cigarette and motioned for me to stand. He pulled two Michelobs out of the ice chest I'd been sitting on and handed me one.

"Plenty of people vow revenge when someone hurts them—"

"Against Pablo Escobar? Shit. Your old man loaded his arsenal into the DC-3 they'd used for smuggling and flew south. Nobody ever heard from him again."

The contents of my father's brown notebook played through my mind. Currito's revelations clarified much of it, and I had a pretty good idea what must have happened next. I hesitated, afraid to ask, but after all Currito had shared it was silly to hold back.

"Los Pepes?"

His eyes narrowed and became hidden behind smoke floating up from his nostrils.

"*Los Perseguidos por Pablo Escobar.* It was a bloodbath," he said. "Anyone who'd worked for or helped Escobar was targeted. Many were murdered no different than he'd killed his enemies. Entire families were killed, political guerrillas, even cops who'd helped Escobar. It was a bloodbath, I'm telling you. They fixed what a decade of rule-followers never could."

"Could my father have helped Los Pepes?"

"Who knows, kid? For all anyone knows he might have led the effort himself. He was that determined."

"That's crazy. I knew my father too well to believe—"

Currito sat forward quickly, his index finger like a dart that hit my father's picture holding the machine gun like a bull's-eye.

"If that's your old man, Buck, everything I told you is true." He stared hard into my eyes and then sat back. "But you believe what you want."

I took a swig of the beer—choked, coughed—but forced the mouthful down.

Several moments of quiet ensued, each of us no doubt recalling very different memories of the same man. I cleared my throat. A sense of claustrophobia tickled the urge to flee, but I had a couple more questions to ask.

"What about Frank Graves?" I nodded toward the photo. "Did he fly south for revenge, too?"

Currito took a long drag on his Parliament, sat back and watched the smoke lift toward the ceiling of the covered porch.

"I don't recall the details of what Frank was doing then. But he got busted with a load of grass in Gautier, Mississippi, not long after Charlie disappeared. Was the last load any of those boys ever ran, and Crazy Charlie only showed up here in Key West one more time, far as I know."

"Only once?"

I thought of vacations we'd taken here when I was young and of the picture on Shark Beach. I'd decided not to share that with Currito. If all this was true, my father did have some serious balls coming back here to vacation under a completely different identity. Why would he have done that?

"Couple months after he left. Nobody knew why. He just appeared one day and was gone the next."

"You said Graves did twenty years?"

"Their luck had run out. Tommy getting killed, your old man going berserk, Frank getting busted—it was over. Times changed and the power in Colombia shifted to Cali. New relationships and routes were used, and, well, it was messy."

"Why didn't Graves turn evidence against my father? Help save his own ass?"

"Maybe he did—everyone thought so—since your old man disappeared, too. We figured he was either in jail or took on a new identity and vanished." A dry laugh parted his lips. "Can't believe he became a big wheel in the State Department. That nobody ever recognized him. What a perfect rebirth."

I took the cell phone out of my pocket, did a quick Google search, picked one of a hundred pictures and held it up for Currito. "Charles Reilly Jr. Undersecretary, Department of State. That was his official photograph."

Currito took the phone, donned his reading glasses, and held it close. After a few seconds of scrutiny he looked up at me.

"Son of a bitch, it *is* Crazy Charlie. Unbelievable."

6

"WHY IS IT SO QUIET HERE TODAY?" I said.

"The airport's officially closed, Buck," Ray said.

We were there on the tarmac and had the cowling on Betty's port engine open. Ray was cleaning each of the spark plugs.

"Irma's running up Cuba's northern coast like a buzz saw," he said. "Category 4, winds still at 150 miles-plus per hour."

"Any change in the Bermuda high?"

"Not budging. I don't think there's any chance the storm will turn north or even dip south. She's coming right at us."

"Shit."

"We have one more family to evacuate," Ray said.

"I've lost track how many times I've flown junk and people up and down the coast. I'm exhausted. Can you handle it?"

Ray was silent.

"Ray?"

"That last trip down, Betty backfired and spit a lot of oil. I need to figure out why so we can get her out of here before the storm. There's no room in any of the private hangars here—I checked."

"Most people evacuating are long gone. Who booked the last-minute charter?"

"Local fishing guide. Pepe Gonzalez and his family. They were planning to hunker down until the latest projections made it clear Irma was headed for the Keys. Two cute kids, Buck. Pretty wife. Good Key West people."

"They ready to go?"

"Be here in an hour." He held his eyes on mine. "All public services have been suspended. No police, no fire department, no utilities, phones, nothing. This family needs to get out."

For the next hour we removed each of the eighteen spark plugs on the Widgeon's port radial engine, two per cylinder. As fate would have it, in the last cylinder we found excessive oil. Worse, there were metal shavings mixed in with the oil.

"Damn," Ray said. "Must have a bad ring or worse."

"Can she fly?"

"Yeah, but if the piston seizes, the whole engine could catch on fire."

Coming around the corner from the boarded-up aviation terminal were a man and woman holding two large suitcases and ushering two young boys ahead of them. Ray was right—the woman was pretty.

Introductions were made, and I asked Pepe where he needed to go.

"Charleston, South Carolina."

"Too far," I said. "Fuel's short. So is time."

Pepe and his wife exchanged a glance.

"Orlando then." Pepe turned to the kids. "You guys want to see Mickey Mouse?"

"Yes!"

"Okay," I said. "Let's load up." I pointed them toward the Beast fifty yards away.

"I seen this thing flying around here, man. Is it safe?"

"You got better options?"

"I'll drive if need be, brother."

"She's fine, don't worry," Ray said.

Just then an old blue Cadillac pulled onto the tarmac. It swerved a few times before cutting to the left—right toward us. I recognized the antique, its faded paint and the plume of white smoke in its path.

Pepe saw the car and smiled. "The Bail Bondsman? You need a get-out-of-jail-free card or something?"

"Go ahead and buckle your family up in the plane," I said.

Currito pulled up next to Betty.

"Excuse me, sir," Ray said. "No cars are—"

"Relax, Waldo. The airport's closed," Currito said.

"You looking for me?" I said.

"I found an old friend of Crazy—um, your father."

"Crazy who?" Ray said.

I took Currito by the elbow and steered him toward the Beast. Pepe still stood on the tarmac next to the plane. He and Currito exchanged nods.

"You found Frank Graves?"

"Close. His ex-wife. She knew your old man, too. They was all thick as thieves—or smugglers anyway."

"She know where Graves is?"

"What am I, a private eye now?"

"I just thought—"

"She called him a piece of shit, so I don't think they're—what's the word—amicable."

"She remembers my father, I take it."

Currito cackled. "Anybody who knew Crazy Charlie would never forget him."

"Do me a favor and stop calling him that," I said.

Currito shrugged. "She lives in Old Town and is willing to see you. Today."

I glanced toward the Beast. Pepe raised both his hands as if to say, *What's the holdup?* Ray had to put Betty's port engine back together. I had to get this family north.

"I have a charter. Short trip. I'll call you when I get back."

"Make it quick, cuz. Wouldn't keep that tough old broad waiting. And this storm's looking rough."

The round-trip flight to Orlando consumed the balance of the afternoon. The Gonzalez kids were well-behaved, though they did climb around the cabin of the Beast like it was a jungle gym.

Once on the ground in Orlando, I realized I was in close proximity to Winter Park, where Craig Dettra had told me Scarlet now lived.

There was a private phone room in the FBO. I closed the door and dialed the number.

"Hello?"

Scarlet's voice momentarily caused my throat to constrict. I hadn't spoken to her since she'd been my patron angel in the British Virgin Islands, where she'd found critical evidence to prove that I'd not killed the man I was moments away from being convicted of murdering.

"Hey, stranger."

"Buck? Is that you?"

"The one and only. I tried calling you in Washington last week. Craig gave me your number, said you're divorced?"

"I am," she said, "but I'd rather not talk about it."

Her voice was distant—how could it not be, given our history?

"I'm sorry, Scarlet. I shouldn't have called—"

"Don't be silly. I'm happy to hear from you."

Her tone emboldened me. "Would you have any interest in researching a family mystery set in Colombia in the 1980s and into the nineties?"

Another pause. "What family?"

"Mine."

"Intriguing. That was a fascinating era there, but I'm afraid I can't. I'm pretty busy these days, Buck."

What a schmuck. I don't talk to Scarlet for nearly ten years and when I do, I ask for help. Again.

"Of course. I understand. Foolish of me to think—"

"Relax. I'm not put out by your request. I'm flattered. We were quite a team back in the day."

"The best."

"But I'm not in that business anymore, and I try not to look back."

"I understand."

"Are you still in Key West?" she said.

"Headed back there now—I just dropped a family off in Orlando who evacuated in case the storm hits the Keys."

"Get out of Key West, Buck. Irma's headed that way. I have friends at the Red Cross who are already gearing up, which is tough since Harvey has them spread thin in Texas."

"I'll be careful."

"Good to hear your voice," she said. "We're overdue on getting together and catching up."

Scarlet was on my mind as I flew back down the Keys at sunset. She'd been so integral to my life at e-Antiquity—my success—that she'd even dubbed me King Buck. Hell, she was the glue that held e-Antiquity together. I'd ruined all that.

No cars were visible on A1A below me. It was like the road had been condemned or a mysterious plague had extinguished the inhabitants of the Keys. The horizon to the southeast was black. The front line of the storm was approaching. Within forty-eight hours, it would either make landfall in the Keys or—please God— pass us by.

I reached up, tapped the throttles forward, and felt the vibration of the dual radial engines increase. The tachometers were as close to redline as I was comfortable pushing them. The storm approached, but it would not deter me from going to see the former Ms. Graves tonight.

SECTION 2

THE SINS OF OUR FATHERS

7

RAIN PUMMELED THE SIDEWALK AS I RAN fifteen feet from the front door of the La Concha to Currito's Cadillac, which was parked on Duval Street. The door opened with a screech and I dived inside, soaked.

"Jeez, the freaking rain is coming down hard," I said.

The car didn't budge. "This ain't even the outer bands of the storm yet," Currito said.

"What's the latest news?"

"Jim Cantore predicts a ten- to thirty-foot storm surge."

"The guy from the Weather Channel?" I said. "That's the kiss of death."

"He's a jinx. Was filming up by the Pier House."

I glanced over my shoulder and saw only blackness. "We going to Frank's ex-wife's house or not?"

"She lives four blocks away. Relax."

Currito put the old Cadillac into gear and the transmission slipped when he pressed on the accelerator pedal, causing a momentary delay until the gears caught. There wasn't another car on Duval Street. The shops were boarded up, the plywood on one painted with orange graffiti: "Go away Irma!" Another said, "Looters will be eaten."

Currito turned the giant Cadillac onto Fleming Street.

"Her name is Eleanor. She moved here in the mid-seventies from South Carolina, I think. She was a waitress at Fitzgerald's at the La

Concha when Frank met her. She was fine back in the day. Haven't seen her in years. Wonder if she's still fine."

The rain smeared the glass to the point where I couldn't see through it. Currito drove with one hand on the wheel, the other clutching a Michelob pony and a Parliament clenched between his fingers.

Rain blurred the street signs, but he turned the Cadillac onto what I assumed to be Elizabeth Street.

"She lives on Solares Hill. Lucky for her it's the highest point on the island."

Moments later he pulled up in front of a house, a classic old Conch design painted white with green shutters closed up tight—the only house on the block with the porch light on. Currito took a final drag on his cigarette and killed the bottle of beer. He honked the horn once. A moment later the front door opened.

The silhouette of the woman in a doorway was wide. So wide she blocked all light except for what spilled out above her head. I glanced at Currito, who had leaned toward me to peer out my window.

"That her?" I said.

"Damn."

A piercing whistle shrieked out above the rain.

"That's her. She always whistled like that to get Frank's attention when he ignored her. Used to make me want to jump out of my skin."

"Let's do this," I said.

My door shrieked open and I lit out across the sidewalk, up the steps, and onto the porch. The rain stung my back.

She didn't speak, but she studied my face. Hers was weathered and wrinkled from a life in the sun. No makeup, not even lipstick, and her hair hung around her face, limp and straight down to her shoulders.

Currito shuffled in after me, slipping on the pine floor. I caught his arm and prevented him from landing on his ass.

"Shut the door!" she said.

Currito obliged. They stared at each other. A short cackle emanated from deep inside her throat.

"Been a long time, bondsman."

"Damn, girl," Currito said. "Can't believe you been living here all these years and I ain't seen you."

"I don't get out much."

My quick survey of the room provided all the explanation I'd needed to understand why. Every inch was filled with piles of junk except for a narrow path down the hallway and into each room. Newspapers, magazines, Tupperware, shopping bags, abandoned appliances, figurines, sets of glassware, and Mr. Z's pizza boxes were all stacked from floor to ceiling. Copious items pressed in on us from every direction. Eleanor Graves was a world-class hoarder.

I caught Currito's expression as he seemed to come to the same conclusion.

"Damn, girl. You got a museum here or what?"

Her expression was hawklike as she turned from him to me.

"I don't see any resemblance," she said. "Come back here where the light is better."

She brushed past me, pressing me against a newspaper pile, and disappeared into the labyrinth of rubbish. I hesitated—Currito pushed me in the back.

"Let's move, cuz. This shit's fascinating."

8

WE WERE SEATED AROUND A SMALL DINING-ROOM table surrounded by more boxes and heaps of junk. It shrank the room to a space we could barely fit into, and Eleanor took up the majority of that. The heat of her breath was a sour breeze across the narrow table. Currito was jammed in next to me on an old church pew.

"We all assumed Charlie was in jail," Eleanor said after I told her I was adopted. "Or dead."

"Yeah, well, this is all new to me, too. I had no idea he ever lived in Key West or what business he was involved in."

Eleanor shifted her attention and squinted at Currito.

"I've known Buck—Charles Reilly III—for nearly ten years," Currito said, "and never had a clue they were related until a few days ago." He turned to me. "Show her the pictures."

I squeezed my shoulder sideways around Currito and pressed against a stained Jack Daniel's box to reach into the breast pocket of my fishing shirt.

"My parents died ten years ago, but I just found these in my father's personal effects."

I put the photo of my father and his two friends on the table, followed by the one of him shooting the guns. Eleanor picked up the one of the three men.

"That's Charlie, all right. Along with Frank and Tommy." She paused. "Must have been in 1988 or 1989. Wow, this really brings me back."

"When did you and Frank get married?" I said.

She squinted at me over the photo and then dropped it and picked up the one of my dad shooting.

"I've seen other photos from this day. Frank and Tommy took them. They loved their damn guns. Dumb-asses." She dropped the picture.

I wanted to ask if I could see other photos, but I wanted even more to keep her talking, so I stayed quiet.

"Frank and I got married in 1993. May twenty-first," she said. "He went to jail a year and a half later. For twenty years."

"When was it Tommy got killed in Medellín?" Currito said.

"Fall of '93. Then Charlie went to Colombia—for revenge—and we never saw him again."

Sweat trickled down my back and my shirt stuck to my skin. I wanted to ask for water but didn't want to break the moment.

"Currito told me Charlie worked for the State Department. What the hell? That was a shocker."

"Believe me, it's just as shocking to learn of his life before that," I said.

"I looked him up online this afternoon. Sure enough, that was him. Older, but it was Charlie all right."

"Do you know where I can find Frank?" I said.

Eleanor leaned forward and rested on her forearms. "Did you find any notes or information in Charlie's—your daddy's effects, as you called them—to indicate where their stash might have been?"

"Stash?"

"I forgot about that," Currito said.

"What do you mean?" I said.

Currito leaned sideways so he could look straight at me.

"Tommy and Charlie supposedly stashed a lot of cash. Nobody ever found their money—"

"Frank was a partner, too—"

"To be accurate, Eleanor, Frank was the muscle of the operation, not a partner."

She glared at Currito for a moment, then turned her weasel eyes toward me.

I concentrated on returning her stare. "I didn't find anything about a stash." The map I'd found in the brown notebook was just a map, right?

"Frank lied to me back then," she said. "Puffing himself up like he was some kind of tycoon. I'd have never married the moron had I known how stupid he was. All brawn, no brain."

"Plenty people got busted in those days," Currito said.

"He had no business trying to step into Tommy and Charlie's shoes. They had the connections, they knew twenty different off-loading sites, and they had everything greased. Dumb-ass Frank gets himself busted on the first try and spent twenty years in jail." She shook her head. "Made me a laughingstock and got me banished from my family back home. Been stuck on this damned rock ever since."

In this house, by the look of it.

"Do you know where I can find Frank?" I said.

Her eyes squinted. "He's around the lower Keys. This'll blow Jade's mind, that's for sure."

"Jade?" I said.

"Oh yeah," Currito said.

"Tommy's daughter. About your age. She's searched for the mythical stash ever since she was a kid."

"What about Jade's mother? She still here, too? She must have known my father."

"Died of drinking when Jade was a kid."

"Jade still live here?"

"Last I heard she was tending bar at the Green Parrot."

A gust of wind rattled the hurricane shutters. An image of flood-waters raging through the junk-filled house gave me a chill. Eleanor would never escape.

"Are you going to evacuate?" I said.

"Hell no," she said. "Where would I go?"

We thanked her for her time. She grimaced. Currito and I squeezed through the rubbish, caught our breath under the balcony, and dashed headfirst into the storm. Inside his Caddy, he lit a cigarette while my mind spun from the séance with Eleanor Graves.

"Jade Diaz is a fox, cuz," Currito said. "Used to be a dancer—so I was told." He pumped his eyebrows.

"I'll look her up," I said.

Currito waited for me to smile, but I wasn't showing my hand.

A stash?

The torn map in my father's journal might lead to something after all. Provided I could figure out what the notations of the maps indicated. Especially if others had been searching for the stash since the '90s.

One thing *I'd* never searched for was a drug smuggler's cache.

9

I WAS THE ONLY OCCUPANT LEFT IN RESIDENCE at the La Concha. Lindy Kramer, the maintenance man, jumped up when I entered the lobby. Lindy was normally hunched over a broom—I'd never seen his tall skinny frame stand so tall.

"The hell you still doing here, Buck?"

"That's a damn good question. Can't say I planned to ride the storm out, but one of my planes can't fly and Ray's taken the other and won't be back until the coast is clear. Just us here, huh, Lindy?"

"'Fraid so. Boss made everyone else leave, but he's paying me time and a half to keep an eye on things."

Built of masonry and concrete in 1926, the La Concha was as solid as anything in these islands. The windows had been replaced with hurricane-rated glass and frames, so Lindy and I would be as safe here as anywhere.

"I got access to the restaurant, fridges, and freezers. Boss said eat whatever I want." He smiled, showing his two missing front teeth. "So we got food."

"You staying in a room on an upper floor?"

"Almost high as you. I'm on five."

With that I was on the elevator and, moments later, in my room. Had the La Concha ever been down to only two inhabitants? Maybe during Hurricane Wilma in 2005, but that was the last major Category 4 or 5 storm since the Labor Day storm of 1935 that destroyed Henry

Flagler's railroad and killed hundreds in the Keys. I felt a twinge of guilt at having been so critical of the weathermen and meteorologists who a week ago had projected Irma would hit Florida.

I took Dad's journals out of my backpack, having retrieved them from the Beast's locker when I returned from dropping Pepe's family. I turned the pages—I'd memorized several names and the chronological data, which tracked exactly with Los Pepes' activities in Colombia I'd found online. Eleanor had confirmed that my father had gone to Colombia for revenge in the fall of 1993 after the Medellín Cartel killed his partner, Tommy Diaz. The last cluster of dates and names of Los Pepes' victims were in late 1993 and into 1994. Escobar had been killed on December 3, 1993.

I lay down, my head spinning. Rain streaked the windows as if garden hoses were aimed at the glass.

I awoke twenty minutes later and slumped into my chair with the brown notebook. This time I started from the back. The torn half page pulled at my imagination. Why was it torn? What was missing? Did the two pieces lead to the smuggler's stash?

A flash of lightning was followed seconds later by a crashing boom.

I flipped on the television, tuned to the Weather Channel. Radar images of the storm covered northeastern Cuba. The text box in the corner of the screen indicated winds blowing 155 miles per hour, the storm moving twelve miles per hour, and pressure at 925 millibars. The next line I read hit me like a kick in the groin.

"505 miles ESE of Key West, FL."

"Jesus."

Quick math indicated that at that speed and path, Irma could reach Key West in forty-two hours. The phone rang—I jumped.

"I'm here at Spruce Creek. The Beauty's in Ron's hangar."

I glanced back at the TV. "Good."

"Ron asked when you'd be here with Betty. Told him about the problem with the port engine."

"Sucks," I said. "Any luck with securing a hangar at EYW?"

"Nothing's available. I double-tied Betty down before I left." I didn't respond. "You could drive your Land Rover up the Keys."

"The news says the gas stations are bone-dry all the way up to central Florida. The Rover's a gas hog."

"You should have left with me—"

"Okay, Ray. I told you I had an important meeting. I'll be fine. Just take care of the Beast. Last Resort Charter and Salvage needs at least one plane to stay in business."

Silence was loud on the line.

"Be smart, Buck. Stay inside."

I laughed. "You know me. I always play it safe."

"Yeah, and pigs fly."

We hung up and my mind closed in on another idea.

I glanced at my old Rolex Submariner.

It was six fifteen—as good a time as any to see if Tommy's daughter still worked at the Green Parrot. With my rain gear on, I stepped out the back door of the hotel to where my red bike was locked on the rack. The rain had lightened some and the wind wasn't too bad as I pedaled down Whitehead for two blocks to the corner of Southard Street. Lights were on inside the Parrot and music played through the open-air windows like on any other night, imminent hurricane or not.

With any luck, Jade Diaz would be there to pour me a rum.

10

THE GREEN PARROT HAD MAYBE twenty customers. Some were at the bar and others played pool while eating free popcorn. Music was loud on the jukebox. I'd been here enough times to recognize a bartender with bushy brown hair and a handlebar mustache, who looked at me like I was a total stranger.

"Pilar dark, neat," I said. I glanced around as I peeled off my rain gear and noted some familiar faces from around town.

My drink appeared. "Cash or tab?"

I didn't have any credit cards, a side effect of my bankruptcy after e-Antiquity crashed. Sufficient time had passed for me to apply for credit again, but I'd gotten used to living lean and wanted to keep it that way. I handed him a twenty. And given my mission, I had to modify my standard operating procedure and make an impression.

"Keep the change."

That earned me a raised eyebrow and a sharp nod. "Thanks, man."

"Parrot staying open through the storm?"

"Depends on how things go."

I downed the rum in one swallow.

"I'll take another, this time on the rocks."

The drink appeared. I gave him another twenty with the same instructions and he nodded again. He lingered, so I leaned closer.

"Jade still around?"

He glanced at his watch. "Better be here in fifteen minutes. I need to get up to Cudjoe to board up my trailer."

I toasted him and sipped the rum.

Perfect.

The rum numbed my tongue as I swirled it around my mouth. I knew nothing about Jade Diaz other than that our fathers were drug-smuggling partners. I couldn't say that about another human on Earth. It gave us a unique kinship—at least in my eyes.

I killed the rum and switched to Coors Light. It was half gone when an athletic woman ran inside from the Southard Street entrance. She shook her hooded jacket off and a mane of wavy blond-tipped brunette hair spilled out around her shoulders. She walked to the restroom.

"That beer's on me," the bartender said. "I'm out of here soon as Jade's finished in the head."

"Good luck on Cudjoe, man," I said.

Jade appeared—tanned, fresh with faint lipstick, no other makeup. She had on khaki shorts and a T-shirt that showed off nice curves and a flat stomach. Her legs were muscular and her feet were clad in Birkenstocks. She was pretty but not of the cover-girl variety. She lifted the counter hatch and entered the bar.

Jade shared a brief conversation with the bartender, who whispered something, nodded toward me, and left the way Jade had come in. A couple of people on the other side of the bar ordered drinks and I watched her move. Comfortable behind the bar, she quickly fulfilled every request but did not seem rushed. She worked her way around the bar and glanced at my empty cup.

"Another beer?"

"Coors Light, please."

She put it on the bar a moment later and leaned closer. "Heard you were asking about me."

I smiled. "Yeah, I think we may have some friends in common."

"Unlikely. Six bucks for the beer."

Shit.

I put a twenty on the counter, but she'd already moved to another customer.

That was smooth, Reilly.

The smell of popcorn had me hungry, but I wasn't budging. I killed the beer so she'd come back. I slid the empty cup to the inside edge of the bar and pulled the twenty back so she'd have to ask again. Ten minutes passed before she came by and nodded at the cup.

A full beer was on the counter within a minute.

"I'm Crazy Charlie's son," I said as she began to pivot away.

She spun on her toe like a ballerina.

"What'd you say?" Her face was tight, like she'd just been cussed at.

I swallowed. "I'm Crazy Charlie's son. Our fathers were partners here back in the late eighties, early nineties."

Her eyes widened and she stared at me for a full thirty seconds before her eyelids fluttered. I held my breath the entire time.

"No shit."

"Can I get a rum and Coke over here, please?" A voice shouted from down the bar.

"No shit," I said.

"Never knew he had a son." Her expression remained wary.

"And I never knew he was in the business, back in the day."

A slow smile briefly bent her lips and white teeth peeked out of her mouth. "I'll be damned."

"Hope not," I said. "I was counting on comparing notes."

She glanced around the bar. There were maybe ten people left.

"I'm closing early, at nine."

I glanced at my watch. It was a few minutes after seven. "You evacuating?"

She shook her head. "Nope."

"Me neither."

"So?"

"Grab a bite later?"

"Sure," she said. "Lucy's is open until ten o'clock. You know the place?"

"Grinnell between Carolyn and Eaton?"

"Yep. See you there."

No amount of rain could wipe the smile off my face. Jade would be a wealth of information. And she was a treasure hunter.

11

LUCY'S WAS HALF FULL, which, given the oncoming hurricane-cum-mandatory evacuation notice, was remarkable. It was a combination of Conchs and fresh water wannabes eating and drinking under the thatched ceiling decorated with the vibe of a West Coast surf shack. It probably wouldn't have mattered if the style were a Swiss chalet theme or a Polynesian *hukilau*. People still on-island wanted to eat and drink, and Lucy's was one of the only places open.

I arrived at eight forty-five with the express purpose of choosing a table that would provide privacy. I settled on one past the empty bandstand in the narrowest and least populated part of the restaurant. When the harried waitress finally arrived, I ordered a jerk chicken appetizer and fish tacos we could share, along with a Bitter Blond—Pilar blond rum, bitters, and ginger beer—to quench my thirst. A lone dark figure walked up Grinnell Street, hood pulled tight, a wraith against the dark rainy night. The figure hesitated in Lucy's open doorway and then shook the hood back. Jade's dark wavy blond-tipped locks fluffed out to shoulder length. She acknowledged my wave.

My drink arrived.

"I'll take one of those," Jade said.

Her attention turned to me, her eyes searching mine. This time I held my tongue, which wasn't easy.

"You say you're Crazy Charlie's son," she said. "Got any photos?"

I smiled. "Fair enough." From inside my breast pocket I removed the photo of our fathers with Frank Graves.

She studied them, glanced up at me a couple of times, and handed them back. "Not much of a resemblance."

I held the photo of the three men up and compared Tommy with his daughter. He'd been a dark handsome man with high cheekbones, a rakish mustache, and a cleft chin. Jade, seated across from me and watching my every move, was a dark beauty with high cheekbones and a cleft chin.

"You, on the other hand, look like your father's daughter."

"When were you born and where?"

I dug into my pants pocket, removed my money clip, and presented my Florida driver's license. "I was born in Washington, D.C. My parents adopted me when I was a baby."

Jade grinned. "I didn't think you looked like the pictures of Crazy Charlie I'd seen. Your parents still around?"

"They were killed in a hit-and-run accident."

"Sorry." She paused. "Now you live in Key West and are crazy like the rest of us for staying behind." It wasn't a question.

"We used to vacation here when I was a kid—"

"So weird—"

"And when I lost my business—"

"e-Antiquity?"

I studied her face. "Must have been quiet at the Green Parrot for the last hour."

"Didn't take much effort. Plenty online about Buck Reilly—Charles B. Reilly III, that is."

"Ancient history."

"Sounded like a reincarnation of Crazy Charlie to me. And now you run Last Resort Charters?"

"And Salvage. That's right. Out of the La Concha Hotel."

"Pretty pricey there. You inherit a pile from your old man?"

I took a gulp of rum. "Guess you didn't read far enough. My brother inherited everything—long story, but suffice it to say I came here with nothing more than an antique airplane." I hesitated. "An old friend of my family has connections with the company that owns the La Concha. I have a special deal."

"And your father somehow metamorphosized into an undersecretary of state? From what I've heard about him, that seems beyond improbable." Her drink arrived. She held it up for a mock toast and drank a long slug.

"Guess we're both in shock. I'd have never believed Dad was into anything illegal—much less drug smuggling—had I not spoken to a couple of reliable sources."

"Eleanor Graves? I'd hardly call her reliable."

"Currito Salazar."

"The Bondsman? How do you know him?"

"We go back a ways."

Her pinched lips relaxed and her eyebrows lost their arch. "I'll ask him about you."

"Do what you need to do. Like you said, there's plenty about me on the Web, but you on the other hand pretty much don't exist."

"How I like it." A brief smile followed.

"Me, too, but as you found, I can't escape my past. By the way, did you run a classified ad in the *Citizen* asking anyone with information about a Charlie Reilly who lived here in the eighties and nineties to e-mail the Citizen?"

"Nope."

The food came and Jade dug in. She radiated confidence with every move and every word. I liked that. You know what you're getting with people like that. Or they're really good at hiding things.

"Everybody who knew your father thought he must have been killed," Jade said.

"Like yours was? I'm sorry for your loss."

"Never really knew him." She swallowed a mouthful of taco. "I was a baby when he died."

"I haven't learned much, but it seems they were quite the dashing pair, our fathers."

"Living *la vida loca*," she said. " Your father became a government big shot. My father was murdered."

"Am I supposed to feel guilty because mine wasn't?"

Our eyes held for a long second. I drained my Bitter Blond.

"Another drink?"

"I need to go soon. Not done getting my house ready for Irma. So you just found those pictures and got curious?"

"Pretty much."

"He didn't leave you anything else? Mementos from those days?" A new light danced in her eyes.

"I found a few other things of interest," I said.

"Such as?" She leaned closer.

I rested my elbows on the table. "You first, Jade."

Her brow furrowed. "What's that supposed to mean?"

"From what Eleanor said, we have more in common than our fathers' having been partners."

She cocked her head. A nervous pang ran through my gut. I didn't want to blow this.

"So?" she said.

"We're both treasure hunters."

She sat back. Her jaw was clenched, but I couldn't tell if she was angry, torn, or both. She finally sat forward.

"Lot's of people who grow up in pirate towns like Key West are treasure hunters, Buck."

"They don't all have half a map," I said.

A long few seconds played out between us. My drink and check were put on the table and the waitress said something, but neither Jade nor I looked up. She finally licked her lip again.

"What map?"

"We both have to get ready for the storm," I said. "Let's sleep on this conversation and meet for coffee in the morning."

"Coffee? There's a killer hurricane bearing down and you want to meet for coffee? Yeah, you're Crazy Charlie's son, all right."

"If we're going to work together, Jade, it has to be a two-way street. Our fathers were partners—maybe we can be, too."

"Yeah, well, we know how that worked out, don't we?"

I put cash on the table for the check and drank the cocktail down.

"Fine," she said. "Let's meet at Five Brothers at eight. Just down the street from here."

"See you then."

With that Jade stood, pulled her hooded Gortex jacket on, tucked her dark hair inside, gave me a last look, and walked out.

My mind spun with possibilities as she disappeared into the blackness.

12

"HURRICANE IRMA LOOKS CATASTROPHIC." Ray Floyd's voice sounded over the speakerphone in my room. "You're better off flying Betty out of there—"

"You said the piston could seize and the entire engine could catch fire."

"True, but that still might be better than leaving her at risk on the runway."

"Thanks, Ray. I appreciate your concern—"

"Damn right I'm concerned. Have you seen what that storm did to St. Barths? St. Martin? The Virgin Islands? I'm telling you it could be cataclysmic."

"How's the Beast?"

"The Beauty's fine. Nestled snug in Mr. Weiner's deluxe hangar—there's room for Betty here, too. So when can you leave?"

That depended on whether Jade had the missing half of the map. And if so, could we quickly figure out the maps based on what we collectively knew and still evacuate before Irma hit?

"I may be able to get out of here tomorrow afternoon or Sunday. Depends on a breakfast meeting I have tomorrow."

"Breakfast meeting? The storm's projected to hit Florida on Sunday morning, Buck. It may already be too late. You should leave at first light—"

"Not happening, Ray. Let it go. The meeting is important."

"Is it worth your life? Or Betty's? What the hell?"

"I'm on to something—"

"Can't it wait until next week?"

The reality was that maybe it could, but I couldn't. All right, wouldn't.

"I don't expect you to understand—"

"What the hell's wrong with you?"

"Take it easy, Ray—"

"Easy? You know how hard I've worked to get Betty back in operable condition? We're partners now, Buck. You said so—"

"I'm meeting her early in the morning. We'll see how it goes."

"Her? You're staying for a girl?"

An irritating static crackled in my ear.

"Jade's not just a girl—"

"Did you say *Jade*? There used to be a stripper at Bare Assets named Jade—"

"Back off, Ray. That's enough. I'll check in with you in the morning after my meeting—"

"You're a fool, Buck. They're talking—"

I hung up. What can you say when you know exactly what someone's going to say and you know they're right?

The chairs in front of Five Brothers were full of older men, some black, some Latino, others Caucasian, and their laughter could be heard a half block away. I cruised up on my bike and adjusted my backpack, and they quieted down. They watched me like I was an apparition.

"Storm coming, son," an old bald black man said. "Might want to pedal yo' ass north."

A murmur of laughter followed.

Jade appeared on foot at the far corner and walked across the street. She had a purse slung over her shoulder. The men all got quiet as they watched her approach.

"Hey, Ms. Jade," the same man said.

"Morning, Freddy. Gentlemen."

"Coffee?" I said.

The man named Freddy looked at me and whistled.

She pushed the door open and walked past me. I ignored the peanut gallery and followed her in. The bodega was small, two aisles and the food counter. Jade was already engaged in conversation—in Spanish—with the man behind the counter. There was an elaborate coffee system to the barista's right. He spoke in a short burst, then nodded.

"What are you having, Buck?"

"Double Bucci, please."

"Sugar?" the barista said.

I nodded. The man nodded, too, and got to work. Jade moved to the back of the bodega, where we were hidden by shelves stocked with Cuban foods.

"We slept on it—now what do you have to tell me?" she said.

I glanced around. Someone was visible through a small opening behind the counter that led into the kitchen. A young guy with glasses leaned on the cash register, twenty feet away.

"Here?"

The man put two coffees on the edge of the counter. Jade walked over, gave the cashier money, and returned with them to where we stood next to a counter-high table.

"Eleanor and Currito both said you searched your entire childhood for a stash," I said.

She didn't blink. "So?"

I swung the backpack off my shoulder and laid it on top of the white counter in the middle of the aisle between the racks of Cuban sundries. She stared at the bag. I unzipped the main section, reached inside, and removed Dad's brown notebook. She stared at it so hard I wondered if she had X-ray vision.

"I found this among my father's oldest possessions. It contains many lists of names. Most are Colombian, some Cuban, Nicaraguan, Panamanian, and all dead." She glanced up sharply. "I assume you're familiar with Los Pepes?" My voice was a whisper.

"Those persecuted by Pablo Escobar, the murderous bastard. Sure." She licked her lower lip.

"The names and dates start after your father was killed in the fall of '93."

Her eyes wandered for a moment, a faraway stare that lasted a few seconds.

"Why would your father have that list?"

"I don't know for sure, but word is he went to Medellín to avenge your father's death."

She took a step back and I intuitively reached toward her. She slapped my hand away and leaned against the back counter. I allowed her a minute to process the information.

"I want to see the list."

"I'll make you a copy."

"Now—"

"Your turn," I said.

I inhaled a deep breath. We both sipped from our coffees, hers a large *con leche* and mine a double espresso.

"That list doesn't have anything to do with—"

"There's more," I said.

She took another sip of coffee. "My father also kept notes. Not in a fancy notebook but on calendars and random pieces of paper. He left a dresser full of crap." A small grin lifted the corners of her mouth. "Took me years to make sense of it, but I finally concluded he'd left us—me—a message."

"Do you think he knew we'd meet?"

"I meant Mother and me, asshole."

I felt my face flush.

"Your turn," she said.

I had my hand on top of the brown notebook.

"I found a hand-drawn map."

Jade stepped closer.

"It piqued my curiosity, but until I learned about you and your hunt for a stash here, I didn't understand why."

"What do you mean?" Her voice was hoarse.

"The map was torn in half. I'm willing to bet that you found the other half in your father's dresser."

She took in a short breath, stared at me, and crossed her arms. "Let me see it."

"Let me see yours."

She laughed unsteadily and glanced around the room. Others had come in and were waiting in front of the coffee counter as the barista made magic with his machinery.

"You're full of shit," she said.

"You got yours with you?"

"Don't push me!"

I let a moment pass and killed the Bucci, and the caffeine accelerated into my bloodstream. People stood waiting for breakfast and coffee while Jade's hyperventilating chest gradually slowed.

"Look," I said, "you haven't been able to solve this by yourself, and maybe, just maybe, I have the missing key—just like you might have for me. Together we may be able to figure this out. Our fathers were partners—yours was murdered and mine helped bring Escobar and his cronies down. It'd be justice for us to work together to figure this out."

"Justice, right."

"Look, I'll give you a good-faith glance of my map. Only a flash, though. Then you can decide. Okay?"

She looked around again but leaned in closer. I could smell her hair. It had the scent of papaya, mango, and coconut.

"Well?"

I picked up the notebook so only I could see inside, found the page, and checked to make sure nobody was watching. Then I swung it open to the torn page.

Her mouth immediately dropped open. I immediately slapped the book closed.

It took her a moment to look back up at me. She actually smiled at me.

"I have the other half."

"Show me."

"Not the original," she said. "But I have a copy of it."

My heart raced, whether from the discovery, the Cuban jet fuel, the beautiful woman smiling at me, or all of the above.

"If you have a copy," I said, "who has the original?"

"Frank Graves."

13

JADE AND I MADE PLANS TO MEET IN an hour at the Banana Café on Duval Street. She said she'd bring the other half of the map but claimed it was a very poor copy.

I rode my bike up Southard to Duval in the rain and crossed over—there wasn't a car in sight, something I'd never seen before in Key West. I turned onto Whitehead and then cut into the side lot at the La Concha.

Even with my rain gear on, I was soaked to the skin. Once inside the hotel's back door, I shed the suit and shook it off so as to not make a mess for Lindy. The hotel lobby was empty—again, something I'd never seen.

Back in my room I changed into dry clothes and checked inside my weather-free backpack for the waterproof pouch that contained my father's notebook, which, of course, was still dry. I didn't like the idea of keeping the notebook with me, but the small room safe I had here was already packed tight.

When I got to the lobby I found Lindy at the reception counter.

I swung the backpack off my shoulder. "You mind if I put this under Susie's desk?"

He held his out toward her office.

I stowed the bag under the desk and jogged down the back hall. The weather had turned too foul for my bike, so I took my Land Rover 88. I'd have been driving it already, but the windshield wiper on the driver's side barely functioned and the one on the passenger side was manual. There was no traffic, so I could drive—very slowly and without regard for things like traffic lights. I made it to the Banana Café, surprised at how fast the trip had been, considering, and even more surprised by all the lights that were on inside.

I parked out front and hurried in.

"Buck, over here."

It took two scans of the room before I saw Jade wave from the far corner. She was with an older man.

What the hell? My business was with Jade. Who the hell was this guy? The man scrutinized me as I approached.

"Who's your friend?"

The man stood. He was nearly as tall as me at six foot three, had a barrel chest, solid legs, a beer belly, a week's worth of beard, and white close-cropped hair. He raised an eyebrow, gave me a quarter smile, and stuck his hand out.

"Name's Frank Graves. Knew your father."

Oh shit.

"Buck Reilly." I glanced at Jade, who smiled as if we were having a family reunion.

"Frank heard about you from Eleanor. I found him waiting at my house when I got home from Five Brothers. He wanted to meet you."

"Your old man turned into some kind of fancy diplomat?" Frank's face twisted up like balled paper. "Don't sound like the Crazy Charlie I knew."

"I guess some people change."

Frank made me nervous. No, it was more than that—I didn't like him. Maybe it was his long stare, or the veiled edge to his voice, or his stance back on his rear foot with his body sideways. It reminded me of my boxing days when an opponent was getting ready to launch his best shot.

"Some got killed, some went to jail," he said. "And one became a big shot."

"Grab a seat, boys." Jade summoned a waitress. "This weather has me hungry."

She ordered a Nutella crepe, Frank black coffee, and me a double espresso. When the waitress left, Frank donned a smile.

"I'm so damn glad to know Charlie didn't get killed down in Colombia. When word got back that our old partners had killed Tommy, Charlie snapped. Vanished the next day." Frank gurgled out a sarcastic laugh. "Left me hanging with a load on the way, but that's another story."

"Turns out Buck's been living here for years," Jade said. "And his daddy used to bring the family down here on vacation when Buck was a boy."

"How 'bout that. And nobody ever knew. What years were those?"

I sat back and decided to play it friendly even though my gut said not to trust Frank. I gave Jade a side glance and she mouthed, "Sorry."

"Would have been over twenty years ago, maybe twenty-five when we last came as a family."

Frank held his hands in front of him and drummed his fingertips together. "Hmm, I would have still been in jail back then. Guess he couldn't of looked me up even if he wanted to."

"My father never mentioned that he once lived here, and I never would've dreamed he'd have been involved in … that business."

"Go ahead and call it drug smuggling, son. That's what it was. And your daddy was the best. A master. Believe me 'cause I was right there with him."

"I still can't believe it's true." I couldn't help but lean closer. This man knew my father in a way I couldn't even imagine. He saw my eyes light up and smiled.

"Go ahead, Frank. Tell Buck some stories." Jade lifted her chin toward me and then gave Frank a warm smile.

"Where to begin? Well, now that we've all met, we don't have to do this all at once, know what I'm saying? We can get together more often."

"How did you and my father meet?"

"I knew Tommy first. Jade's dad. He was half Colombian and had a lot of family down in Medellín. That's how we got started. We'd run a couple trips of grass, nothing huge, but we were getting a reputation. That was in the late seventies, early eighties." He paused for a couple of seconds. "Then, in the mid-eighties a trip got busted and we lost our crew. Your daddy was a bouncer at a local disco. Fact: it was located in the lobby of the hotel where you live. The La Concha."

My mouth dropped open.

Frank laughed so hard it turned to coughing.

"That is too freaking weird," I said.

"Tell me about it," Frank said. "Anyways, we had a big brawl there one night with the family members of shrimpers—our former transporters who'd got busted—and Charlie came to our rescue. He was a cracker from up north and didn't really know better. We was heavily outnumbered, so he pretty much saved us from getting our asses kicked."

Jade's food came along with our drinks. Frank sipped his coffee, a pleased look on his face. I sat on the edge of my seat waiting for him to continue.

"When the disco closed, we took Charlie to the Chart Room bar to show our appreciation. Needless to say, we hit it off. Charlie was a talker—"

"So true!"

"And before long he talked about places he'd lived and people he knew up along the coast in northern Florida, the Panhandle, Louisiana, and remote locations only God knew about."

I clenched my teeth but maintained a grin. My father had never lived in any of those places as far as I knew.

"You all right, boy?"

"Yeah, this is, ah, just new to me, that's all."

"Those old times all run together now. But soon after that night, days, maybe weeks, Charlie started in on wanting to be part of our operation. Mostly with Tommy 'cause he had the connections and they'd hit it off. My role was to bring the muscle for unloading and loading. The Keys was hot with DEA by then, cops from all over, FDLE—you name it. Since our last load got busted, we was extra cautious. We didn't know if any of the shrimpers had ratted us out, so we was keeping a low profile."

"That's around the time my parents had me, then got married," Jade said. "My mother was from New York and had come to the Keys on spring break, met my father, and never left. Same old story."

"Anyway, we needed a fresh approach, so Charlie's idea of moving the deliveries north made sense, and damned if it didn't work like a charm." Frank shook his head and smiled.

"How many trips was my dad involved with?"

"Damn good question. One the cops would like to have known the answer to when I got busted, believe you me. Something like fifteen, easy. Maybe more." He leaned forward. "About halfway into those the product turned to snow."

I sat back.

"Like I said, once this damn storm passes, we got all the time in the world to tell stories."

A nervous twitch began in my left eye.

Frank started tapping his fingertips together again. "Then it all turned to shit. Tommy was down south tending to business and got killed, and Charlie up and disappeared. Word was that he turned into a vigilante and wreaked havoc on those bastards from Medellín."

"Los Pepes," I said.

Frank looked surprised. "Yeah. That's right."

"Buck says he found a list of names tied to Los Pepes in his father's belongings."

"I heard how your parents died from getting run over," Frank said. "Shame about that. In Switzerland? Odd place."

I took a drink of water.

"Among other things, one of the problems was that both Tommy and your daddy disappeared without telling anyone where all the money was. Money we owed the cartels—both in Medellín and Cali—'cause Tommy was in the process of shifting suppliers. My money and what I owed our men for the previous few trips disappeared, too. Needless to say, it was a mess."

"Sounds like it."

"I was left to figure it all out, but that wasn't my specialty."

My stomach tightened. Frank chuckled.

"They used to talk about their hidey-hole like it was some kind of wonder of the world. Nobody could find it, everything was safe, and nobody had anything to worry about. And you know what? Damn if they weren't right. Still nobody's found nothing." His eyes turned to slits. "Unless your daddy retrieved it all during those family vacations of yours." I swallowed hard. "That how he bought that fancy farm in that horse town?"

I held my hands up. "Look, Frank, this has been an amazing revelation. I do look forward to hearing more in the future, but one thing you need to know is that the majority of the money my parents had was from investing in my company, e-Antiquity. They cashed out before we tanked—"

"Lucky for them."

"Yeah, well, not so lucky for me and the rest of us. I lost everything, filed bankruptcy, then they got killed. Long sad story, but the point is, whatever money he—or Tommy or you for that matter—hid away, I don't think he ever touched it."

Jade had been quiet but was on her elbows leaning over the table, intent on every word. I held my breath and wondered if she'd mentioned the map.

"So my question for you, Charles B. Reilly III, is what else did you find in your daddy's possessions? Any clues to where the missing money might be?"

I killed my espresso. "Nothing like that. Just some old pictures and a list of people killed by Los Pepes. I don't know if he was like a fan keeping a box score, or, hell, maybe he was involved. I don't know."

Jade's expression remained inscrutable. We all three sat back. Frank's eyes never wavered from mine.

"That's too bad. Could have been a happy ending after all these years."

My gut said not to trust Frank, and it was nearly always on target.

"I'd asked Currito Salazar if you moved back here after getting out," I said. "And he wasn't sure. This is such a small island—where do you live, Frank?"

"When I came back I wanted nothing to do with anyone I knew back in the day. Lived up the Keys. Got me a job at the Butterfly and

Nature Conservatory, where I see only tourists. Nobody knows me, and I ain't looking to pal around with any old buddies."

I was momentarily speechless. The Butterfly and Nature Conservancy? Hard to imagine him there harvesting chrysalises.

"Speaking of which, I need to get on back and finish buttoning up the conservatory before this damn storm shows up." He slid his chair back—the legs screeched on the tile floor. "Still can't believe all this, Buck. Believe me, I do look forward to talking more."

"That would be great, Frank. Truth is, your stories have blown my mind."

"Lot more where they came from."

I watched as he walked out, agile for a man of his age and size. Then I turned to Jade.

"What the hell? That was insane. I didn't know what to say—or what you'd told him."

Jade pushed her plate away, the crepe half-eaten.

"I know. I'm sorry."

"What about the other half of the map? You said Frank has the original, but what about your copy? Did you bring it?"

She shook her head. "I couldn't get it. He was waiting for me at my house."

"So you guys are close? He comes over to visit?"

She took in a long breath and exhaled it fast. "Frank was like an uncle to me after he got out of jail. I was like his researcher as we tried everything to figure out his partial map. We always thought there might be another part."

Crap.

"Okay, Jade, cards on the table. Meeting him and hearing all that was so out of the blue, I wasn't going to just pull my pants down and say, *Hey, look at this!* Are you going to tell him what I showed you?"

She shook her head. Slowly. "No, but if we find something we should give him a share."

"Right. Okay. But let's not get ahead of ourselves. I can't tell you how many people I've seen at each other's throats over fictional treasure."

The waitress rushed over and dropped the check on the table. "Sorry, folks, we're closing. Now. Bad news."

"What's wrong?" Jade said.

"Storm's turned north. It's coming right at us."

14

THE RAIN WAS EVEN HEAVIER NOW. We stood in the door of the Banana Café and watched water stream down Duval Street.

"That's my truck," I said. "You need a ride?"

"That old Landy?" she said. "Run better than it looks?"

"Not really."

She glanced up and down Duval. "No need. I'm parked around the corner." We exchanged cell phone numbers. "What are you going to do?"

"Going out to check on Betty—my plane—make sure she's tied down tight. You?"

"I'm headed to the Parrot to see how storm prep is going there."

"When are we going to meet and compare notes?" I said.

She looked away. Guilt over Frank? "How about this afternoon? I can tell you what Frank and I have done over the past few years. Where we searched, what we think the clues are on our—his—half of the map, I mean."

"Okay."

We agreed to meet in the lobby of the La Concha at one.

The roads on the way to the airport were already flush with storm water from the outer bands of Irma. Waves smashed up on White Street Pier, and I imagined Atlantic Boulevard getting swamped under storm surge.

The windshield wiper on the driver's side moved so slowly I drove at a snail's pace.

Surf pounded Smathers Beach. There was a kite surfer bouncing off waves—but the waves were so close together that he jumped over several at a time. Crazy bastard.

A sign at the airport said it was closed. Police cars were stationed out front. I continued past and drove to the end, parked close to the Private Aviation building, zipped up my coat, donned my hood, and ran for it. The terminal was locked. I scrambled for my keys, and by the time the door was open I was sopped. No point in rushing now.

Out the back door I leaned into the wind and rain that now came in sideways. Visibility was down to maybe two hundred feet. I spotted Betty—but saw her port wing lift a couple of feet.

Shit.

Ray had double-tied her down, but the lines apparently had come loose due to the fierce wind.

"I'm sorry, girl. I should've flown you out of here."

Betty's hatches were locked tight, and I saw no evidence of water inside as I peered in the window. I cinched the tie-down straps as tight as they'd go.

"I'll come check on you, I promise," I said, patting the underside of her nose.

On the way back to the FBO, I noticed Ted Thompson's De Havilland Beaver with floats he used for Fort Jefferson trips rocking in the wind. I tightened his lines, knowing he'd do the same for me. By the time I got back into the Rover, I looked as if I'd gone swimming fully clothed. My old Rolex Submariner told me it was nearly noon.

The waitress at the Banana Café said the storm had turned north toward Key West. I could have checked the weather report at the FBO—Fixed Base Operations—but headed back toward the La Concha to dry off and check the Weather Channel instead. I parked close to the hotel and once inside again shook my wet jacket off. A number of locals were now in the lobby seeking shelter from the storm. No sign of Lindy, so I retrieved my backpack from the office and took the elevator to my room.

As soon as I lifted my key toward the hole, I noticed scratches on the lock and the wood door.

Shit!

From my backpack I pulled out an eight-inch Buck knife. If someone had broken in and was still inside—

I turned the key, heart pounding, and shoved the door open.

No one inside, but the room was trashed, every drawer dumped out. The room safe had been pried open and its contents dumped onto the floor, too.

Had to be Frank Graves. There wasn't much of value here, and of that, nothing appeared to be missing.

The Butterfly Conservancy, huh?

Time to pay Frank a visit.

I sheathed the knife, and put it back in my backpack. Then I considered my options. What to do with my father's notebook, which was open to the page with the torn map? I hesitated and then carefully pulled the map out of the binding. I folded it and put it inside the small orange waterproof pouch that already held my wallet and cell phone. The pouch fit snugly in my breast pocket.

Every inch of the floor was covered with my possessions. I dropped the notebook into the middle of the pile. Hidden in plain sight.

Fucking storm—fucking smugglers—fucking Dad—fucking Frank.

The elevator hit bottom and I ran out into the lobby. I jogged past the counter and was turning into the back hallway when I heard someone shout my name.

"Buck! Stop!"

I spun on my heel—Jade rushed toward me.

"Where are you going?" she said. "Thought we were going to meet at one o'clock!" She stared into my eyes, which must have looked crazed given the startled look in hers. "What's wrong?"

My teeth were clenched so tight it took a moment to loosen my jaw.

"Buck, what happened?"

"Somebody—Frank—trashed my room."

"Frank? Are you sure? Why would he—"

"Did you tell him about the map?"

She took a step back. "No, I told you I didn't—won't. Why do you think it was him?"

"Who the hell's left on this rock? Who the hell has a reason to look for something in my room?"

"That's why I'm here." She patted the pocket in her raincoat. "Is there somewhere we can go to compare notes?"

She smiled at the sight of my brow roll up.

"My room's destroyed." I glanced around. The lobby was too crowded with locals. There was still no sign of Lindy. "Follow me."

I walked behind the check-in counter and into the small private office. Once inside Jade closed the door behind her. The room was cramped, and the smell of rain and perspiration combined with Jade's coconut-scented hair to create a complex bouquet. I pushed the contents of the desk to one side.

"What do you have?" I said.

"Give me a better look at yours, first."

"I already showed it to you once—"

"For a half-second."

"Okay, then let's do it like the game of war."

"What the hell's that?" she said.

"You know, the card game? Means we flip our cards over at the same time."

Her lips puckered for a moment. "Okay."

She dug into her jacket pocket and removed a clear plastic sandwich bag. As she carefully unzipped the seal, the lines and size of the paper caught my eye. While the paper was more yellowed and worn, it looked like the partial map from my father's notebook.

"Where's yours?"

I smiled and unzipped my jacket and removed the orange pouch from my shirt pocket. As I pulled the paper out, her eyes widened, no doubt at the same recognition I'd experienced when I saw her half of the map.

We both held the halves of the same page up—mine an original, hers a copy—the side with the map details invisible to the other, ready to lay them down on the table.

"You do know how silly this is," I said.

"Shut up and play war, Buck."

We slapped our papers down on the desk face up.

15

Each half was a perfect continuation of the other. The jagged tears on each side fit together like puzzle pieces. Jade stared at my map, and I could see her eyes follow each line: the tree-shaped symbol, the three half-squares on the right side, and a long line that ran parallel to the tear with a circle next to an oval that bled off the tear.

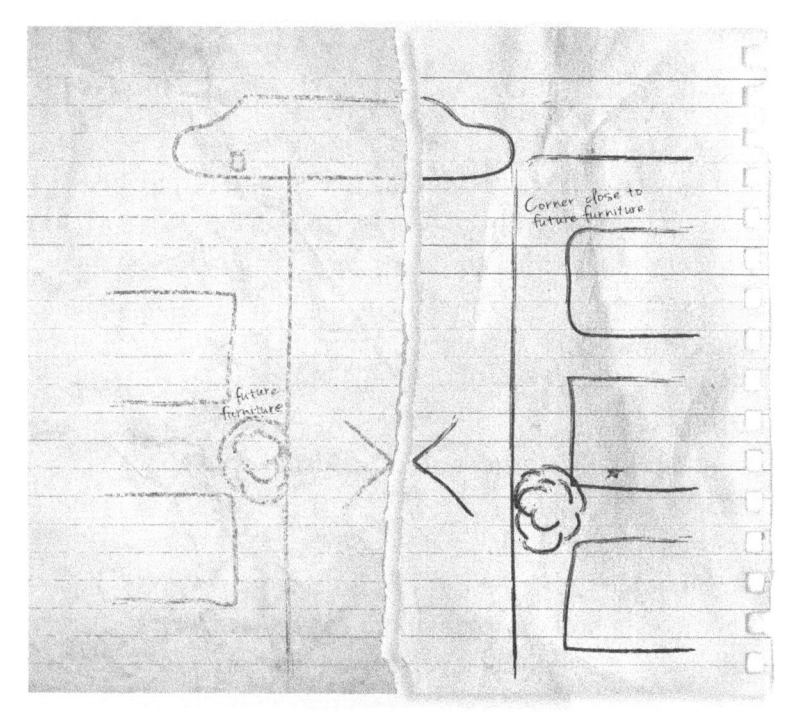

What I thought was an arrow on the middle edge of my page also appeared on Jade's, but hers faced the other way. I slid the pages together and the two arrows formed an *X* in the middle of the road.

I glanced up at Jade.

On her page I noticed that the same oval from my map continued but was much longer. There was a small box toward the left end. Hers also had a long line that ran parallel with the tear of her page, another tree-shaped squiggly circle, and two rectangles on the left side.

It was a street scene for sure. The long parallel lines were two sides of the same road. The oval was … who knew?

And what was the *X*?

"*X* marks the spot?" Jade said.

There were some small faint handwritten notes on both maps. Mine said "Corner close to future furniture," which meant nothing to me. I leaned in closer to see the writing on Jade's, by the tree.

She pointed to a squiggly line that said "Future Furniture."

"I'm assuming that's a tree, so what kind of wood could it be?"

"I've always assumed it's a mahogany," she said.

"So the tree is cut down—in the future—and made into furniture."

"Not if the city's Tree Commission has anything to say about that."

"So we need to look at all the mahogany trees—"

"You know how many mahogany trees are on this island?"

"But how many are directly across from each other?" I pointed to the same squiggly shaped circle on my map. "And assuming these boxes are houses, we need to find this pattern."

"What about the cigar-looking shape?" she said.

"Hard to say, but if we find the trees and house pattern, we'll see what's there."

The door to the manager's office suddenly opened.

"Buck?" Lindy said.

I stood up fast to block his view of the desk.

"Hey, Lindy, yeah—by the way, you see anyone lurking around earlier? Somebody broke into my room and trashed it."

"I ain't seen no—trashed? You got robbed?"

"Didn't really take anything, but yeah."

"Oh, man. Jeez, I'm so sorry. Damn, I'll get fired—"

"It's not your fault, Lindy. I think I know who it was."

"Oh. You sure?"

"Yeah, I'm sure. Mind closing the door, Lindy? We'll be out of here in a couple of minutes."

"Damn, damn, damn." The door closed slowly and clicked shut.

"So you didn't have any other information with the map?" Jade said. "Street name? Address? Nothing?"

"Zilch. What about you? Just the other half of the same map?"

Jade nodded, and then we each retrieved our maps. She placed hers in plastic and I put mine inside the orange pouch.

The door opened again.

"Sorry, Buck, forgot to say why I was looking for you."

I waited.

"Ray Floyd called and wanted me to find you. Word is Irma's gonna nail Key West—with a direct hit. He pleaded—asked me to plead, too—that you get Miss Betty out of here." Lindy looked at Jade. "That you, ma'am?"

"That's my plane, Lindy."

"Oh, that must be why he said the airport'll get devastated, storm surge will likely be from ten to thirty feet, and, well, Miss Betty'll likely get washed out to sea. Sorry, Buck."

The door closed behind him.

Crap.

"How about I fly us off the island?" I said.

"In Betty, I take it?" She let out a long breath. "Would be the smart thing, but …"

Now that Jade had seen my father's map, she really didn't need me anymore. So I wasn't surprised at her reaction to my suggestion.

"I'm not leaving," she said.

"Why not? We could search when we return—"

"Eleanor Graves, that's why. She's an old woman—"

"What about Frank?"

"He doesn't care about her. They've been divorced forever. He said he'd check on her, but Eleanor doesn't believe it and neither do I."

"He's too busy with the butterflies? And breaking into my room?"

"I don't know, Buck. Frank and I searched for years and you heard him—he thinks he has a right to whatever's there, too. He's wound tight, but that's what twenty years of prison does to a man."

While Jade spoke, I imagined a wall of water smashing Betty to pieces and pushing her carcass out to sea. Storm surge of ten to thirty feet? Was that even possible here? Another thought caused me to suck in a fast breath.

"Something wrong?" Jade said.

"What Lindy said about the storm surge."

"Scary."

"The maps," I said. "The *X* in the middle of the road."

"What about it?"

"If it marks something buried there or in some kind of cavity, a storm surge of ten to thirty feet would probably destroy it. When was the last serious hurricane to hit the Keys?"

"Andrew was in '92—before my daddy was killed—but there wasn't much flooding."

"What about Georges?"

"That was in the late '90s and ripped through Cudjoe Key with a ten-foot surge. And then Wilma about a dozen years ago, but that didn't flood much either."

"Depending on what they buried and where, if it was high enough to avoid storm surge, then it might still be there."

"And dry."

Jade's face faded to a pasty white. She stood up and fumbled with the zipper on her jacket.

"What are you doing?"

"We need to go see Eleanor. Now."

"Why?"

She licked her bottom lip. "Because I'm pretty sure the middle house on your map is hers."

SECTION 3

DISCOVERIES

16

THE RAIN POUNDED HARD AGAINST THE ROVER'S windshield. Jade manually operated the passenger-side wiper faster than the automatic one on my side, but visibility was maybe ten feet anyway. Fortunately, Eleanor's house was only a couple of blocks away.

"You know this area is called Solares Hill, right?" Jade said. "Highest point on Key West."

I was concentrating on not sideswiping parked cars on the narrow road. "Currito drove me here last time. Which house is Eleanor's?"

"One away from the corner. On the right."

As I approached, my stomach dropped. The houses were close together and there was a large mahogany tree on Eleanor's side of the road, but not one across the street. I parked the Rover in front of the house one before Eleanor's.

"See the mahogany tree?" Jade said.

"Nothing across the street," I said.

She looked and turned back to me with a frown. "Let's go."

We popped the doors open and sprinted up Eleanor's steps until we were under the covered porch. The window shutters were closed but light bled out from inside. News of the storm blared at top volume from the television: "…with maximum sustained winds of 150 miles per hour…" Jade used the knocker to pound on the front door.

A moment passed. She pounded again.

Eleanor jerked the door open, her eyes wild.

"Jade, why are you still here?" she yelled over the weather news. " Irma's coming right for us!"

"I told you I was staying—"

"I told you that was an idiotic decision."

"I tried to get her to leave," I yelled.

"Can we come inside?" Not waiting for an answer, Jade pushed past Eleanor. The old woman slammed the door closed behind us and turned toward me.

"You're Crazy Charlie's son. You two know each other?"

"You told me about Jade—"

"Leave your wet jackets out here."

The TV kept blaring. "Headed directly for the Florida Keys, Irma is—"

"Can you turn that down, please?" Jade shouted.

"What?" Eleanor screamed from the kitchen.

We peeled off our soaked outer layers and I followed Jade into the kitchen.

"… worst-case scenario shows half of Key West underwater …"

Jade pushed the "mute" button on the remote control.

"I was watching that," Eleanor said.

She had three cases of water stacked in the corner, a mountain of canned foods on the counter, a small propane camp stove, and a giant fishing cooler that was probably packed with ice and other provisions. She must have cleaned out Fausto's.

Eleanor saw me eye the pile of groceries. "Cost me an entire month of Social Security."

"How long have you lived here?"

Hesitating, Eleanor glanced at Jade, then back at me.

"Since '95."

"So you and Frank were still together then—"

"He was in jail, but yes, legally."

Something seemed odd to me, as if Eleanor were skirting something.

"Want a bottle of water?" she said.

"You bought it while Frank was in jail?"

"It was my father's house," Jade said.

Her arms crossed, she had a defiant gleam in her eyes, as if it were none of my business. Normally I'd back away from body language like that, but this was different.

"Your father's house? But he'd already been—"

"My mother died in '95. Booze and drugs. She never recovered from my father getting murdered. Eleanor—Frank, really—got the house."

An awkward silence closed in on us.

"Why not you?"

"Frank had papers signed by my father stating that he'd get the house if something happened to him. There was nobody to argue it—I was a kid—so I stayed here for a while before going to live with relatives in northern Florida."

I was confused. "I thought you grew up here?"

"I went back and forth."

"Frank was in jail and I was working," Eleanor said. "We weren't exactly parent material."

Jade took a bottle of water from the case and handed me one, too. It was warm but tasted good. So this was Jade's father's house that Frank had inherited. Something still felt off to me, but I wasn't sure what, other than the two women's visible discomfort.

"This house has quite a history," Eleanor said. "Was owned by bootleggers in the twenties and wreckers before that."

And smugglers from the eighties on. A real den of ill repute.

"Nice mahogany tree out front," I said.

"As long it doesn't crush my house in the storm. Mahoganies have shallow roots. Every time there's a storm in this town something bad happens. I would have cut it down if it weren't for the damn Tree Commission. They care more about old trees than houses getting smashed by them."

"Mahoganies make for nice furniture," I said.

"One across the street sure did."

Future furniture. Jade and I shared a glance.

"Across the street?"

"It was half dead due to illegal pruning. The Tree Commission fined the Shepherds five grand, so they cut it down and made a bedroom set out of it. Darn pretty, too."

Eleanor was actually smiling. Some people got off on anything that turned the tables on power-wielding bureaucrats. The ex-wife of an ex-con was understandably that kind of person.

"Frank said he handled logistics for our fathers," I said.

Her brief sparkle turned dark.

"Logistics? More like muscle." She aimed a rueful grin at Jade. "Probably never told you this, but Frank came here from Oklahoma as a sixteen-year-old. His father was a drunk who used to beat him for sport."

"He fled?" Jade said.

"He fled, all right. They found Frank's father dead, his skull crushed. Beaten to death with a baseball bat."

Jade met my wide-eyed glance without so much as a wince.

"No witnesses and no evidence, so Frank was never arrested." Eleanor glanced from Jade to me. "He never admitted killing his dad, but when I asked, he smiled. I got this house in the divorce while he was behind bars."

"Where's he live now?" I said.

"In a trailer on Stock Island. Must feel like a mansion after all those years in a cell." A raspy laugh followed. No love lost between those two.

"Do you know where my father lived back then?"

A new light lit Eleanor's eyes. "Matter of fact I do." She turned to Jade. "Frank ever tell you that?"

Jade shook her head as if to ask why she should care, and then her brow suddenly furrowed.

Eleanor smiled again. "Back in the day, Crazy Charlie lived in the Shepherds' house across the street."

I dropped my water bottle.

17

JADE TOOK HER MAP OUT AND LAID it on the kitchen counter.

"You still chasing that foolish map you found in your daddy's junk drawer?" Eleanor said.

"Maybe not so foolish anymore. Let's see it, Buck."

I hesitated. The storm was building. Betty could get torn apart sitting out in the open.

"Buck?"

"See what?" Eleanor said.

I vowed to check on Betty again and took the orange waterproof pouch from my breast pocket. After unrolling the flap, I slowly pulled my father's half of the map out and placed it on the counter next to Jade's.

Eleanor's intake of breath sounded like a Dustbuster turning on. "Oh my God, where'd you get that?"

"Buck's father—Crazy Charlie—and my father each kept a half of the map."

"From what I saw, your house, Eleanor, might be this one right here." I pointed to the middle square on the right side of my map. "That looks like your mahogany tree."

She pressed between us, donned her reading glasses, and peered down at the maps. "I'll be damned."

I pointed to the other tree—"Future Furniture"—across the street.

"Is that where the Shepherds' tree was located?"

She edged closer and followed the small squares on her side of the street as if to acclimate herself. Then she went straight across to Jade's map.

Her finger stabbed the bottom square on the map closest to where the mahogany had been. "That one right there." The note on my map said "Corner close to future furniture."

I pointed to the same square. "That was my father's house?"

Eleanor nodded. Her eyelids blinked repeatedly.

"If this is Angela Street"—Jade waved her index and middle fingers over the lines that ran the length of the tears in both maps—"then what's this oblong thing that cuts across the road? Elizabeth Street's another house away, and there's nothing visible there."

We both turned to Eleanor, who, to my surprise, smiled. "Old-timers used to say that back in the Prohibition days, bootleggers who lived in this neighborhood dug tunnels between houses to stash booze, this being the highest point on Key West."

Jade and I locked eyes.

"Maybe that cigar-shaped-looking thing is a tunnel."

Maybe. But if the box-shaped square on the left side was a tunnel entry, what was the *X* that had been intentionally bifurcated in the middle of both pages?

My palms were sweating, and that familiar treasure tingle in my gut had my right eyelid twitching.

Eleanor started to laugh.

"What's so funny?" Jade said.

She went on for a minute. "You and Frank," she finally said. "All those years, it was right under your noses."

"Hilarious, Eleanor, thanks."

Jade's relationship with Eleanor was a mystery to me. Maybe it was Frank she was closer to and the divorce and obvious disgust Eleanor had for her ex-husband was a wedge between them. Why couldn't Eleanor have cared for Jade after her mother died? The old woman's bitterness had deep roots.

"If that's a tunnel noted on the maps and if that's a hatch," I said, "it looks like it's right in the road. The city would have paved over that several times by now. No way they'd have ignored something like a hatch."

"Let's go have a look," Jade said.

"At least your new partner really is—or *was*—a treasure hunter." Eleanor laughed. "Maybe you'll find some dried-out dope Frank could peddle so he can spend the rest of his miserable life back in jail."

Jade and I reclaimed our maps and put on our soaked raincoats, which were pointless really.

"That old woman has always been such a bitch," Jade said once we were on the porch with the door closed behind us.

"You said you stayed behind to take care of her?"

Jade gave me a long cold glance. "You love all your relatives?"

"I don't have any relatives left except my brother, and we don't get along."

"Too bad," she said. "You think Eleanor's right about a tunnel?"

"Not sure. 'Close to future furniture' suggests it has something to do with the corner of my dad's old house. That being said, let's go have a look at the cigar shape."

I was resoaked before I made it to the bottom step. A wind gust hit me and blew me a step off course. I righted myself and we leaned into the wind and crossed the narrow road. A sodium vapor light on a pole near the corner provided illumination, and we paced the far side of the road from the corner and back. As I suspected, there was nothing visible in the pavement. No hatch, so square shape.

"The oblong extends onto the property here," I said.

We walked all around the front yard of an old single-story shotgun house that was pitch-dark inside. Sidewalk and landscaping covered every inch of the lot that the house didn't occupy.

"We'd need a backhoe to find anything here."

"I don't know what that's supposed to be on the maps but I'm not wasting time on Eleanor's suggestions," Jade said. "Let's go look at your father's old house."

Even before she said that, I'd been staring at the dark two-story, double-porch home. It was a classic-Key West style painted pink with burgundy shutters. I doubted that had been my father's choice.

Rainwater had filled my shoes, and the fierce wind made me shiver even though it was hot and humid.

The house was empty. The Shepherds must have evacuated. Sensible people.

Something caught my eye.

"Look at that." I pointed to a wide stump from an old tree cut close to the ground.

"Future furniture," Jade said.

We turned and looked back at the house. I focused on its corner. The note on my map had referenced that. Amazing.

Jade was staring back across the street toward Eleanor's house. I pictured our fathers—the young dashing men in the pictures I'd found of them—walking across to see each other, hatching plots, organizing smuggling operations. It must have been hell when Jade's father was killed. I imagined Dad standing here after that, staring at his friend's house.

Not hard at all to imagine his going to Colombia for revenge.

"How about the mark near the corner of Eleanor's house on your map?" Jade said. "What do you think that might be?"

The mark she referred to was either a smudge or a star. I hadn't paid much attention to it, but clearly she'd memorized every detail. There was no doubt in my mind that had I left to evacuate Betty, Jade would be standing here right now trying to solve the puzzle.

"Let's go check it out," I said.

18

BACK ON ELEANOR'S PORCH, WE CONSULTED my father's half of the map.

"There, see that? What's that mark?" she said.

"Let's assume it's an *X*, albeit smaller than the one torn in half in the middle of our combined maps."

We were out of the rain now, but water still blew sideways under the covered porch.

"Based on the placement, the map takes into account the porch here, Buck. Otherwise, the square shape of the house would be further back from the road's edge—"

"If we're right and that's Angela Street," I said, "then that's something marked under the corner of the porch there." I nodded to the left corner of the porch. "You never played under there as a kid?"

"Why would I play under the house? There are scorpions under houses here."

"They're not lethal to humans."

"Some are."

"You'd think Frank would have gotten under there for some reason—"

"Frank was in jail. And Eleanor couldn't fit under there even if she wanted to ... The porch is about three feet off the ground. Let's crawl underneath and check it out."

"Not worried about scorpions?"

"Thought they weren't lethal." Jade rolled her eyes. "I'm going to ask Eleanor for a flashlight."

"I'll find a place where we can climb under."

Jade knocked on the door as I descended into the deluge. The wind buffeted me and the rain pelted my face, but I was used to them by now. I dodged some scrubby untended bushes and walked between the mahogany tree—its branches noisy—and the edge of the porch.

Around the side, the once-green lattice that ran the perimeter of the house and covered the crawl space was faded and chipped. Between two overgrown bushes was a dead one, and I grabbed its trunk close to the ground and pulled hard. It came loose and I fell backward and landed on my rear end.

Behind where the dead bush had been, the lattice board was rotted and leaned inward. I kicked it and the board fell flat inside.

A light was shone in my face from above.

"See anything?" Jade said.

"I found an opening in the lattice where we can get underneath. Bring that light and let's go."

A moment later Jade was next to me. I reached for the flashlight in her hand, but she brushed my arm away.

"Follow me," she said.

We crawled slowly on our knees under the porch—there was roughly three feet of clearance between the house and the ground. The flashlight beam illuminated coral gravel spread evenly under the house, which rested on coral piers placed in a twenty-foot grid that provided clearance for floodwaters.

It was pitch-black except where the light beam was aimed. I tugged on Jade's pant leg in front of me.

"Aim it over here in the corner."

The light revealed a low, bulky concrete foundation.

"Is that the cistern?" I said.

"I can't tell."

"Hold the light there and I'll check it out."

My knees dug into the jagged coral as I crawled forward. The concrete structure, which had a lid, definitely looked like an old cistern, but that was what any concrete box would look like in this setting.

"Hand me the light."

As I leaned closer and aimed the light onto the structure's surface, a burst of adrenaline coursed through my chest and arms. There was an old metal handle and a spring-loaded hinge on the front edge of what looked like a solid concrete lid. There was a hoop on the side with a clasp that ran through it. A lock might have once been there, but nothing was bound to the clasp now.

"Will it open?" said Jade, who'd scurried up next to me. I handed her back the light.

"Keep it pointed on top."

My hand cast a long shadow as I reached in front of the beam and took hold of the handle. I pulled up—hard. It didn't budge.

I tried again, harder this time, but still nothing.

Still bent over, I got from my knees to my feet—not easy when you're six foot three—and inched forward with my back scraping against the joist supporting the patio above. Once positioned over top of the concrete structure, which was about thirty-six inches square, I took hold of the handle with both hands, sucked in a deep breath, straightened my arms, and dead-lifted it.

SCCRRREEEEEECCCHHHH!

The lid broke free and the spring-loaded hinge howled like a she-devil roused early from winter hibernation. The lid was heavy. I squatted like a power-lifter, leaned forward into the weight of the lid, and pressed it over toward the front of the porch. Thunder sounded outside after a flash of lightning sent a checkerboard pattern of radiance through the lattice and onto the ground in front of us.

Jade pressed up next to me and aimed the light down into the hole.

"It's a tunnel," she said. "I can't freaking believe it, but it's a tunnel."

I peered down into the hole. The floor of the tunnel was down maybe six feet from where we hovered over it. The walls were made of stacked boards with spikes holding them in place. And there were items down there—crates, maybe?

"Give me the light," I said. "I'll go first."

"Okay, treasure hunter, let's see what we have here."

The light lit the bottom of the hole, which looked to be dirt. Still flat-footed and bent over, I lowered my right haunch onto the thick concrete casing, swung my legs into the hole, and dropped into the blackness, where my feet landed with a thud. Dust launched up around me, and I started to cough and sneeze.

Jade was asking questions before I'd even caught my breath.

"What do you see? Anything there?"

I bent down and aimed the beam into the blackness. Then I stared at the contents and tried to assess what I saw.

"Buck? Buck!?"

19

"WHAT'S DOWN THERE, DAMMIT!"

I shone the light up through the hatch. "Come see for yourself."

"How far's the drop?"

"I'll catch you."

A couple of seconds passed—Jade dropped like a bag of potatoes into my arms. For all her attitude, she was light but solid. I held her for a few more seconds.

"Put me down, dammit! Shine the light into the hole!"

I lowered her slowly, and when she hopped from my arms I aimed the light into the cavern. The wood boards that framed the walls and the ceiling were in good shape, with the exception of a couple from the ceiling that hung down. Tree roots had grown through them. The flashlight beam lit a half dozen crates of dusty bottles and some other piles beyond them.

"Is that booze?" Jade said.

"Eleanor said bootleggers used tunnels."

"What's that deeper inside?"

I walked forward, crouched down. The fading light make a faint white pool ahead. I recognized the material on a stack of two box-shaped items the size of hay bales. Burlap. I knelt and poked at the top one with the flashlight. Even though they were nearly thirty years old, the pungent smell was unmistakable.

"Is that weed?" Jade said.

"Affirmative."

A duffel bag was on the ground deeper in the short tunnel. I walked forward and tapped the bag with my foot. It was an old L.L. Bean bag. My father loved anything from L.L. Bean. I bought nearly every birthday and Christmas gift for him from its mail-order catalog. I took a knee and pulled the bag toward me to find the zipper—it was heavy. I felt a large object through the canvas.

ZZZZZZIIIIIIPPPPPPP.

I spread the bag wide and found a Thompson submachine gun inside. With a couple of clips, fully loaded.

"Freaking gangsters, our fathers," Jade said.

"This looks just like the gun my father was holding in that picture of him on the beach somewhere."

"You can have it. What's that underneath the gun?"

I leaned the gun against the wall behind me and pointed the light inside the bag.

It was full of cash. Stacks bound in rubber bands.

"Finally, something worth a shit."

"Not much there," I said.

I dumped it onto the floor and we both picked up a stack.

"This one says $1,000," Jade said.

"This one, too."

I handed them up to her one at a time and she stacked them on the bales of grass.

"All these years searching and we find twenty grand and some old dope?"

I held the light on the wall. There was a drawing on the wall—maybe two feet wide, drawn on the boards with what looked like black marker. A long hat-shaped oval and, on the right side perpendicular to it, a smaller rectangle with rounded ends.

The shape of the drawing gnawed at my memory. I aimed the light to the drawing's left side. A square was drawn inside the hat-shaped oval, almost all the way to the left.

"Is that like the cigar-shaped thing on our maps?" Jade said. She caught on quick.

"Looks like it, but this has more detail."

I ran the light along the perimeter of the shape toward the right. The line was jagged on top in some places, smooth along the bottom. But the lines looked intentional.

I sucked in a breath and nearly dropped the flashlight. "No, it can't be!"

"What? Buck? You recognize something?"

I leaned closer to study the smoother line on the bottom. There were subtle details like hash marks.

"Son of a bitch."

"What is it?"

I started to laugh and shone the light all around the tunnel. I spun in a circle looking for other drawings and laughed so hard my eyes watered.

A sudden slap against my arm stopped me.

"What the hell's so funny?"

"This drawing is the same as the one on our maps. And I recognize it now. I can't freaking believe it, but I do."

"Okay, partner, how about clueing me in so I can laugh, too?"

"Holy shit. Dad ... Jesus he—okay, okay." I smiled. "I told you when my family used to vacation down here?"

"Yeah, so?"

"One time Dad rented a boat and we went out snorkeling. I was maybe nine and my brother five. While my mom was on shore making a picnic lunch for us, we got chased in by some sharks—lemons, I think—which my dad, Ben, and I considered a hilarious adventure. When we lined up to take a family photo with the camera set to a timer, my mom asked what we'd been laughing about. A second before the picture was taken, Ben said we'd been chased by sharks, and the picture caught the moment with my mother's eyes bulging in rage."

"But why were you laughing *now*?" Jade's face was dead serious in the spooky light of the tunnel.

"That's a map of the place where it happened," I said. "My family called it Shark Beach."

A slow smile creased Jade's cheeks—

THUD!

We jumped, and my head smashed against the top of the cave.

"What the hell?" I said.

Dust blew toward us. I aimed the light toward the end of the tunnel and a figure cloaked in black, dripping water and crouched below the entry. A fat revolver, .357 or maybe a .44 Magnum, was aimed right at us.

The dust cleared and I could make out his face.

Frank Graves.

20

"WELL, WELL, WELL, LOOK WHAT WE HAVE HERE," Frank said.

"What's with the gun?" I said.

"You finally found it, huh, Jade? With your new friend Reilly here."

"Take it easy, Frank," Jade said. "There's nothing here worth going back to jail for."

"Maybe, maybe not." He blinded me for an instant with a bright flashlight. "What's all that?" He pointed the beam toward the bale.

"Old dope," I said.

"On top of the bale?"

"It's, like, $20,000, Frank. Go ahead, take a third," I said.

Frank's laugh was shrill.

"And Shark Beach, there on the wall?" he said. "I heard everything you said, Reilly. Lovely story, by the way." He pointed the gun at me. "Tell me about what you referred to as the hat-shaped island."

I was pressed back in the deepest end of the tunnel and blinded by Frank's light. He was now a dark silhouette in front of me. I used my hand to block the beam of light while glancing down at the Thompson leaned against the wall between us.

"Don't even think about it, Reilly," Frank said. "The island?"

"Sorry, I was a kid. It's offshore, and I don't know the name."

"How far offshore?"

"I told you, I was a kid. Not really far, but I don't know exactly."

I'd flown over "Shark Beach" a hundred times. It was 9.2 miles off the northwestern point of Key West and called Woman Key. I had no idea what the square box on the map signified.

"It's just a drawing, Frank. Take all the money here, it doesn't matter to me. Just relax—"

"Don't tell me to relax, asshole. I spent twenty years in stir while your old man became some kind of diplomatic rock star. How that happened I have no idea, but he forgot about me like yesterday's news. After all the money I made him, you think he ever checked on me? Called? Nothing!" Spittle rained down in the light beam.

He took a step closer.

Keep coming, Frank.

"That drawing of Shark Beach is nothing, probably just where they stashed bales—"

"No! Not bales." Frank stepped back. "I knew all the places we stashed bales—hell, I was the one who did it. Jade, turn your light on that sketch."

She picked the light up off the bale and pointed it at the wall.

I took a step closer.

"Stop right there, boy! Don't think I won't shoot you."

The Thompson was three feet away. Was the clip in the gun full? Was there a bullet in the chamber?

Frank looked from me to the sketch on the wall and back.

"Tommy told me he and Charlie had a bunker where they kept our cash safe. *Our* cash. We couldn't use banks, and the Keys were full of thieves and other smugglers who'd rob you blind, knowing you couldn't call the cops."

He moved his light quickly around the tunnel and then turned it back on me.

"This can't be it. There ain't shit down here, dammit."

"No problem, Frank. We can take a boat out there after Irma blows past. Whatever's out there, we'll split it three ways—"

"That won't work."

"Why not?"

"Because this storm will flood the out-islands."

"The islands would have flooded in Georges or Wilma," Jade said.

"Neither of those storms had any more than a foot of flood surge out here. Irma could be ten feet."

"Or thirty, according to the Weather Channel," I said.

"That's right, kid. Or thirty. That's why we're going now."

"*Now?*" I said.

"That's crazy!" Jade said. "We'll get killed!"

"You're staying here, Jade."

"We can't take a boat out in this," I said.

"What makes you think I won't call the cops?" Jade said.

"That's right, Reilly. We're gonna take your plane—"

"We sure as hell can't *fly* in this," I said. "You got a death wish?"

"And you won't be calling anyone, Jade. I'm locking you down here. Your life is my insurance policy."

"No. Please." Jade's voice was a whisper.

Silence.

"There's a problem with cylinder nine," I said. "A bad ring or piston—"

"Spare me the bullshit, Reilly."

Silence again, during which I tried to think what might convince Frank that we couldn't fly. Within five seconds, I concluded that nothing would convince him. And he had leverage.

"If we don't hurry out there and back, Jade will drown with her old man's stash of weed and chump change."

"Asshole!" She leaped at Frank, who moved just in time and pistol-whipped the side of her head. She dropped like a bag of concrete, caromed off the bale, and flopped to the ground, unconscious.

"I know your plane's out at the airport, Reilly. You better hope that old piece of shit can fly."

Frank knelt and put his gun to Jade's head. "Now slide past me, move those bales under the hatch, climb out, and go stand by the porch until I follow. You run or try to pull anything when I climb out, Jade dies. Got it?"

My eyes burned into him. "You're one hell of a guy, Frank. Old friend of the family, huh?"

"Not your family—or hers. Both of your old men left me hanging. Time I get my due."

I squeezed past Frank inches away from the Thompson. Even if I knew it was loaded and had a round in the chamber, he'd shoot Jade before I could grab the gun, much less fire it. Once the cash was pushed off the bales, I restacked them under the entry.

"Good job. Now climb your ass out and wait for me by the porch. Remember, do anything heroic and the girl's dead."

It dawned on me that Eleanor had called Frank. Vitriol from their divorce must have paled compared with getting a cut of the smuggler's stash.

I climbed onto the first and then the second bale—both as hard as rocks—and easily pulled myself out of the hole. I'd have slammed the lid, but he might have been fool enough to kill her even if he couldn't escape until the police came. And anyway, he probably knew the city had suspended police, fire, and other services during the storm.

Frank was tying Jade's feet together with some rope from one of the bales. He'd tie her arms, too, the crazy asshole. If we didn't get back in time and the storm surge was as predicted, she'd drown.

"Get moving, Reilly."

Son of a bitch.

My knees dragged against the coral stone until I reached the opening in the lattice fencing. After crawling out from under the house, the wind knocked me down when I tried to stand. The rain was harder than ever, and huge puddles had formed outside.

How would I fly Betty in this?

And where would I land?

I had to alter this situation before that happened or Betty and I would perish in the storm.

And Jade would drown.

21

FRANK REFUSED TO OPERATE THE LAND ROVER'S MANUAL WIPER, and the automatic one on my side was unable to keep up with the torrent. He kept the bulky revolver aimed at my gut.

"You really want to die? Because that's what will happen to both of us if we try to fly in this storm."

"Weather planes do it all the time. Yours is a seaplane."

"Amphibian." I leaned over the wheel and tried to see the centerline down Simonton. "The fuselages on seaplanes never touch the water. Amphibians are flying boats. They drive in the water until they take off."

"Perfect. We'll drive it like a boat out to the island if we need to. Did some research—must be Woman Key. Flatter than a pancake. Your daddy's bunker'll flood for sure."

At the intersection with South Street, the road was already flooded.

Great.

My old Land Rover plowed through the water, but the buffeting winds shook the box-shaped vehicle like a toy in a dog's mouth.

RRRIIIINNNNGGGG.

"The hell's that?" Frank said.

I removed the cell phone from my breast pocket, hoping—illogically—it would be Jade saying she'd escaped. But the name that appeared on the screen was "Scarlet Roberson."

"Don't answer it."

"She'll have news of the storm."

"No!"

"We need information. If I mention you, feel free to shoot me."

I pressed the green button.

"Buck? Please tell me you're not still in Key West?"

"Hi, Scarlet. I'm still here but getting ready to leave—"

Frank jammed the revolver into my side.

"You can't leave now. The storm's headed straight for you!"

"Still a Category 4?"

"Yes, with sustained winds of over 140 miles per hour. You can't fly in that—Irma is four hundred miles wide!"

"Category 4, 140-mile per hour sustained winds, four hundred miles wide," I repeated, looking at Frank. "How fast is it moving?"

"The National Weather Service says it's traveling at eight miles per hour. The eye is eighty nautical miles from Key West."

I glanced at my ancient Rolex Submariner. It was 5:15 p.m. At that speed and distance, quick math said the eye would make landfall on the Keys between eight and ten tomorrow morning, Saturday.

"Just wait it out, Buck. That old hotel you live in is tall and sturdy. You're on the sixth floor—"

"Hang up, Reilly," Frank said.

"I gotta go, Scarlet."

"Buck, I need to talk to you—see you. I'm driving south from Orlando now."

"Don't come here—"

Frank pressed the barrel of the .357 into my ribs. I pulled the phone off my ear as Scarlet continued to try to talk sense into me. I pressed the red button with my thumb.

"Plenty of time," Frank said.

"It'll be dark in an hour."

"Better hurry then unless you want to land in the dark." Frank smiled. "I looked you up, King Buck. You must be an amazing pilot, given all you've done. Made history even." His smile vanished. "You can handle this."

A1A along Smathers Beach was now a liquid track as the storm pounded the shore and blew beyond the man-made dunes. I pressed harder on the accelerator and drove on the far left side of the road. Nobody else was fool enough to be out driving, much less flying.

Just before the East Martello Tower, I turned into the airport exit—it was closer to the private aviation terminal. I parked by the door.

"Destiny brought us here, Reilly," Frank said. "Karma, even. You can thank your dead father for that. Had he paid me like he should have, we wouldn't be doing this right now. And if we die, the blood's on his hands."

"My dad's dead, Frank. The blood'll be on your hands."

He laughed. "Yeah, that's true. Lead the way."

I led Frank through the private aviation terminal and then back outside. He stayed ten feet behind me with the gun aimed at my back. The rain hit me sideways, and as I fought against the wind I must have looked like another drunk on Duval Street. One of the tie-downs on Ted Thompson's De Havilland Beaver had broken loose and the plane was bouncing up and down on the tarmac. I grabbed the flapping line under the Beaver's starboard engine to cinch it down.

"That's not your plane!"

"It'll get destroyed."

"Keep moving."

Ahead, Betty's wheels were solid on the ground. The lines that held her fast were so taut that they screeched like violin strings being strummed by a madman.

"Unlock the hatch," Frank said.

He climbed inside as I ran through a quick preflight to make sure the flaps were still functioning. Once inside, I started the starboard engine and held my breath as I turned the port one over. How long would it last until metal shavings in cylinder nine or the damaged ring around the piston blew apart? If that happened in this storm, we'd never make it on one engine. Frank stayed back in the aft starboard seat, where he could keep an eye on me. With the engines running, I climbed back outside and untied the lines that held Betty in place.

"I'm sorry, old girl. I should've taken you to safety days ago."

"Who you talking to out there?" Frank said.

"Myself. Relax."

I took a deep breath, reentered the side hatch, and coiled myself to spring at Frank. Now or never. But the first thing I saw was the barrel of the .357 pointed right at my face.

"No heroics, Reilly. When I looked you up, I found out you were an accomplished boxer, too. You're going to see a lot of this gun."

Twenty years in jail had honed Frank's intuition razor-sharp.

I got into the cockpit and my harness as Betty fluttered in the wind. At this point it would be safer in the air, so I added manifold pressure by pressing the throttles forward. I spun the plane around to face west on the taxiway parallel to Runway 9. We were about halfway down the tarmac from the southwestern end.

The winds here were already gusting forty to fifty miles an hour. Normally I'd need two-thirds of the mile-long runway to get up to speed, but the lift caused by the storm gusting out of the south would drastically reduce the distance. A glance back at Frank had me hoping he'd smash his head in the turbulence that awaited us or shoot himself by mistake. But he might just as well inadvertently shoot me.

"Hang on," I said.

I pressed the throttles forward and Betty started slowly into the wind. The RPMs pushed toward their redlines, the wind speed was at seventy-five miles per hour, and she hit takeoff speed in record distance. We lifted off suddenly. In fact everything was sudden. The nose shot straight up—I trimmed the elevators hard—and we stalled—I dropped the nose and retracted the landing gear—and then our angle of critical attack was back under control.

Betty bucked like a prize rodeo bull that had never been ridden as the wind did its best to blow her out of the sky. My hands bounced on the wheel like a rock 'n' roll drummer in a frenzied solo to keep Betty flying straight. Frank slammed around in the back but held the gun firmly.

Lightning was striking—often—and I was piloting a flying target. Rain blinded me, but after a one hundred and eighty degree turn Woman Key was almost dead ahead, and at this speed we'd be there in five minutes.

Betty's instruments were true as I tried to recall Woman Key and the waters around her. The western side of the island was a beach, and fairly rock-free waters led up to her, whereas the eastern side was shallow, rocky and had trees up to the edge. My plan was to land a quarter mile offshore and cruise up to the beach. Fortunately, the wind was coming from the southeast, so technically that made sense. Not that anything about this flight and water landing made any sense.

The altimeter showed six hundred feet and spun counterclockwise as we aimed into the blackness where the island should be.

There!

Lights from the lone house—mansion, really—on Ballast Key, the small bottle-shaped island adjacent to Woman Key, were visible. David Watkowski, a billionaire who chose to live in solitude miles out in the ocean, owned the island. Only the caretaker, Greg Holmes, lived there with him. Greg was a friend I'd helped transport supplies for on occasion.

"I see it!" I could hear Frank's shout over the wail of the wind and the roar of the engines. Then I heard something else: the port engine sputtered.

No!

My intention had been to circle the island once and find the best angle for landing, but the fate of the port engine left me no choice. We had to land now.

I spun Betty into another hundred and eighty degree turn and descended toward white waves that appeared like random patterns on a black background. The island was ahead somewhere. A flash of light from Ballast Key off the starboard wing helped. I pushed the wheel forward and pulled back on the throttles. The RPMs dropped, as did the wind speed.

Waves surrounded us as we dropped into them—and bounced up. Again and again—again—now porpoising—the fuselage hit repeatedly—the wings shaking at adverse angles. *Please don't rip off!*

A loud screech—was that the hull?

To slow our progression in the water, I lowered the wheels—which instantly dropped Betty's nose forward. I reversed the props, and Betty settled into the rocking seas. A faint line of beach was fifty feet ahead of us.

I sucked in air, having held my breath through it all. We hit the beach abruptly—sand and marl flew into the air, and Betty tilted forward. I reversed thrust and we settled back down.

"Damn, that was fun!"

"You're a sick bastard, Frank."

"Don't you forget it."

I reversed the props and alternated power until Betty faced back out to sea. I backed us up as far onto the beach as I could, seaweed, sand, and water swirling around us in the wind. But we'd survived the landing and I'd done my best to position us for a quick escape. Not that I was sure we'd ever get out of here. Or that Betty could make it back if we did.

22

THE WIND WAS STRONGER THAN IT HAD been back at the airport, and the rain-darkened skies had extinguished the meager daylight. Betty was literally crabbing around on the beach due to the tempest's press. I took two anchor lines from the aft storage locker—all under the scrutiny of Frank's gun barrel—and piled them in front of the hatch.

"What're you doing?"

"Securing the plane."

"You have a shovel back there?"

"Nope."

"Flashlights?"

I hesitated. There were two 2,400-lumen rechargeable LED lights plugged in and fully charged. I didn't want to help Frank, but stalling hurt us both. And Betty. I pulled the lights off their wall-mounted cradles and handed him one.

"Ready for anything, aren't you, Reilly?"

"Except you."

Frank smiled, as I knew he would.

I unlocked the hatch and had to lean in to push it open against the velocity of wind. It hit me hard and blasted all the seat cushions around the inside of the fuselage.

When I jumped out onto the beach, I was blown over and caught myself by digging my hand in the sand. The ropes attached to the anchors unfurled in the wind and blew around the beach like kite tails. I attached one to a cleat on the port wing and let the wind push me forward, ducking under the nose. I dug my feet in and tied the other rope to the cleat on the starboard wing. Once both anchors were pressed into the sand and the ropes were as tight as I could get them, I returned to the open hatch, where Frank hovered.

"Based on the map," I said, "the square symbol, or bunker as you called it, is on the far west end."

"Move it, Reilly. Lead the way." Frank had to shout over the wind, which had picked up.

Damn.

But at our backs it hastened our progress—I was practically jogging down the beach. This was the first time I'd set foot on Shark Beach since I was here as a child.

An opening in the thicket of bushes allowed me to penetrate the wall of sharp, scratchy vegetation. The image of the square box superimposed on the island from the wall in the Angela Street tunnel guided my internal gyroscope. It was closer to the beach side of the island than the middle, so I aimed my light at the ground and swung it from side to side like it was a metal detector.

Rotting trees and freshly downed ones kept me from taking a straight course, but I was able to get in to where I thought the square on the map had been located.

Nothing. If there was anything to find, it wasn't here.

Disappointing Frank at this point would not be a good idea. I waited until he caught up to me, holding the light steady in his left hand and the gun in his right, breathing fast but not hard. He was fit for a man his age.

"Why'd you stop?"

"Nothing here."

"Keep looking."

"It should be in this approximate area." With that I advanced deeper into the brush, slogged through puddles and standing water, and swung my light around. A machete and goggles would have helped. I walked in a grid pattern, up a hundred feet and back down, a dozen times.

Wait.

It was covered by grass and surrounded by bushes and trees, but I spotted it anyway: a slight square depression in the sandy ground.

"What have you got?" Frank's voice boomed behind me.

"An anomaly," I said. "In my past life, anomalies on the ground increased the odds that something unnatural might be buried below—"

A bright light suddenly shone from the direction we'd come.

"Kill your light!" Now Frank's voice was a low hiss.

The light progressed steadily toward us. The sound of a machete slashed through the brush and lifted my heart.

"Hello? Who's in there?" A man's voice.

It was all I could do to not yell for help.

The light beam suddenly turned to the left, and the man continued on a new course toward the western tip of the island.

No!

He slashed his machete at the vegetation. The light swung back toward us.

I aimed my light toward the man and flashed it on.

"Hello?" the voice said.

Frank swung the gun down on my light and knocked it out of my grasp. It fell into the muck and fizzled out.

"Hello! You okay?"

The light progressed faster toward us now.

When the man was about thirty feet away, Frank raised his light and turned it on, all 2,400 lumens aimed at the man's face—it was Greg Holmes.

BOOM!

Greg fell to the ground. Before I went to him, I yelled at Frank.

"Why'd you shoot him? He's the caretaker from Ballast Key!"

"He was a witness."

I ran to Greg's side. His light blue Patagonia rain jacket was slick with blood. I grabbed the flashlight he'd dropped and turned it on his face. His eyes flickered.

"Greg? Can you hear me? Greg?"

I trained the light on my face.

"It's me, Buck. Can you hear me?"

His eyes bulged wider. Blood streamed from the sides of his mouth and nostrils.

"Why'd you … shoot me?"

"I didn't, Greg. Hang on, man, I'll get you to—"

His eyes opened wider and his head slumped to the side.

"No! Greg—"

"Thank you, Reilly."

I spun on Frank, who, of course, had the .357 Magnum aimed at my chest.

"What the hell for?"

"For getting him over here where I could shoot him. I'd of let him wander off, but this is tidier. Now get over here and start digging up your anomaly."

Thunder roared above our heads, and a lightning bolt struck a tree in the middle of the island, sending flames bursting into the air.

"What am I supposed to dig with?" I said when things got quiet enough for Frank to hear me.

"Your hands."

The wind howled and the rain came down harder.

"Call your ex! Have her untie Jade before she dies!"

Frank laughed. The gun aimed at me didn't budge.

"Dig!"

23

"How do I know you won't kill me anyway?" I said.

"How would I get back to Key West, Reilly?"

I was knee-deep in marl, mud, and water, minus a couple of fingernails from clawing at the dirt, but I'd just felt something solid under the remaining layer of it.

A few more swipes of my now-raw hands and concrete appeared in Frank's flashlight beam.

"What have you got?" he said.

"Looks like concrete. Find a stick or something and give me a hand."

Frank walked toward the far end of the depression, five feet away, and found a wide, flat stick that he dug into the earth, shoving dirt to the side. After a few more swipes he threw the stick to me.

"Use this and hurry it up. Damn storm's getting worse."

I glanced at my watch: 1:15 a.m. The eye of the hurricane was close to the Keys, and the ferocity of the storm had continued to build. It was just a matter of hours before the eye struck and everything in a wide radius would be shredded, flattened, or eviscerated.

The flat stick accelerated my progress, and within fifteen more minutes I'd dug out around the perimeter of the crudely poured concrete. But I'd not yet discovered any type of lid.

"Try the middle," Frank said.

Exhausted but numb to the torrent, I crawled forward like a dog and pawed at the marl with the stick as if on the scent of a bone. Several swipes later, the stick caught on a protrusion: a concrete slab. I used my hands to dig around it.

I felt an indentation in the surface of the concrete and a metal bar that crossed the hole in the center of the slab. In the middle of the bar was a ring.

"I found something."

Frank came closer. I shoved more mud away from the center of the slab, and sure enough, a hatch with the ring over the slab gradually emerged. It was square, roughly two feet by two feet. It reminded me of the lid over the tunnel at Eleanor's house. The rain power-washed the lid. The recess and the rusty ring in the middle became clear.

"Give me a hand?" I said.

"No. Get it open."

I worked my way back up onto my knees and grabbed hold of the ring. The pitted metal dug into my raw hands. I gripped it tight. With white-hot rage at Jade tied up in the tunnel, at being forced to fly a crippled Betty into a hurricane, at Greg's getting murdered, at my father's being a son-of-a-bitching drug smuggler, and at the likelihood of my getting killed tonight, I pulled on that ring.

I leaned backward, using my weight as leverage. The lid popped free and I fell back on my ass flat into the mud.

"Stay put, Reilly."

Frank took a wide berth around me and pointed his light into the hole.

"Oh yeah," he said. "What have we here?"

I felt no joy at this discovery. Just revulsion.

"Aren't you curious, Reilly?"

I remained supine, face up in the mud, as the water pounded my body.

Frank's smile faded. "Curious or not, get your ass into that hole and pull those duffel bags out."

With a deep breath I rolled slowly onto my side. I was too tired to sit up straight—how the hell was I going to stand? I pushed myself up on my knees and somehow managed to stand in the wind. Chills ran up my back, and my arms shook with fatigue and cold. I turned toward the hole. Frank held his light aimed down into it.

It was indeed a bunker, roughly five feet deep. I stepped forward, knelt down, and gazed inside.

I thought of the Thompson submachine gun in the tunnel on Angela Street and another gun in the photo, a nickel-plated revolver that just might be down in the hole. I'd never killed a man, at least as far as I could be sure, but I'd shoot this son of a bitch in a heartbeat if I found a gun.

I slid into the hole and kicked duffel bags around until my feet finally hit the bottom. It was dry. I looked up and saw that I was in up to my shoulders, so the hole must have been about five feet deep.

"Open one of the duffel bags."

With Greg's light wedged in my armpit, I slowly pulled the zipper on the L.L. Bean duffel bag down its length and then grabbed both sides of the canvas and pulled them wide. Frank leaned forward with his light.

The interior of the bag lit up green.

Cash-green.

"That's what I'm talking about," he said. "How many more bags are there?"

I lowered myself deeper into the hole.

"How many bags!" Frank said.

I shone the light around inside the chamber. There were bags everywhere.

"One, two, three, four, five, six—" I kicked one bag forward. "Seven and eight L.L. Bean duffel bags, all of which are probably full of cash." No sign of my father's missing revolver. "Want me to open every one?"

"No. Throw them out. Lickety split. Weather's turning to shit."

Turning to shit?

Each bag was the same color and size, which as I recalled was the largest of the sizes my father favored. They all weighed the same, and I power-lifted each one out of the hole. When there were no more I squatted down for one last look around. My light illuminated some crude writing on the wall—numbers, actually. I stared at them a long moment and recognized them from my father's notebook that contained all the names of Los Pepes' victims.

17000 / 50 # 12000 / 100 # 10,000 / 20 ### LO / SP / EP / ES

What the hell?

I'd previously figured the letters separated by backslashes at the end to spell *Los Pepes*, but the numbers continued to elude me.

A sudden intake of breath sat me up straight. Could it be an accounting of the cash here in the hole?

Fifties, hundreds, and twenties?

"Get your ass up here, Reilly. Time to get me back to Key West."

24

TO MY AMAZEMENT, THE WATERS AROUND WOMAN KEY had literally vanished.

Reverse surge.

I'd never seen the phenomenon but had heard of it happening with especially powerful storms. The disappearance of water had occurred around Thailand after the earthquake there in 2004 only to come back shortly thereafter as a tsunami that destroyed everything in its path and killed thousands of people. Fascinated by the water's disappearance, they'd wandered out into the dry sea basin to see stranded fish, sunken boats, and the exposed undersea world. When the floodwaters roared back, they all drowned.

There had been no earthquake here, so the waters must have been sucked into the storm's vortex. But whether through storm surge or in torrential rains, the water would return just like it had in Thailand.

Hurricane Irma was a beast bearing down on our islands with biblical strength. Locusts or plagues had nothing on this bitch.

Could we escape before the surge rendered our departure impossible? And could we take off across the now-exposed turtle grass and marl sea bottom?

"What if the water comes back in a flood?" Frank said.

"Then we're dead meat."

"Can your plane take off on this shit?"

I walked past Betty into what had been the shallows leading up to the island. My feet sank an inch into the soft sea bottom. There were chunks of coral that could rip a tire clean off the wheel. I did see a path into the dark, but I couldn't see beyond a hundred feet, at best.

It was a suicide mission.

"Are you a praying man, Frank?"

"No."

"Better start."

After three more trips carrying twenty-pound duffels in each hand through Woman Key's scrub jungle down the beach and back to Betty, I could hardly straighten my arms. The rain and wind whipped and howled, sand and debris pummeled my face, and fatigue wobbled my legs. I stumbled.

"Suck it up, Reilly. We have one more load to get from the bunker."

I actually hurried up the beach, fueled less by the fierce wind than by fear. The trip itself might well prove to be fatal, and the chances that we'd make it would be far worse if we didn't take off soon.

Our path through the bushes to the bunker was now well-worn, and we passed directly by Greg's body every time.

"Stop there." Frank's voice was loud.

I turned to face him and winced at the light aimed in my face.

"Drag the body and drop it inside the bunker."

"Why? He's dead."

"No traces. Can't take any chances."

I squinted into the light. Rain swirled between us.

"I'm a trace."

"You need to fly me back—"

"And when we land you'll kill me."

"I'll kill you here if you don't get moving. I can wait until the water returns and sail away if need be—"

"Unless there's a thirty-foot storm surge."

"That's why you're still alive. And remember, we don't get back, Jade drowns in that hole sure as shit. Plus I'm guessing you don't want the world to know the undersecretary of state was a drug smuggler."

Of course, he was right. If the FBI found out, they'd seize all of our family's assets, including the farm in Middleburg.

"I don't need to kill you, Reilly. You open your mouth, you kill yourself." He sighed. "Now drag the stiff into the bunker, grab the two duffels, and let's get out of this hellhole."

Frank held all the cards and the gun. I bent down. Greg's eyes were still staring up. I used the butt of my hand to close the lid on each eye and then grabbed him under the armpits. His corpse had already stiffened in the hours he'd been dead. My legs and back screamed with fatigue, but I dragged Greg deeper into the island, stumbling but never stopping, until finally we reached the opening.

Hunched down, I put my hand on Greg's head. "God bless you, brother. I'm sorry."

When I reached down to grab him by the back of his pants, I found a sheathed knife on his belt. Shielded from Frank, I unsnapped the five-inch blade, drew it out, and slipped it into my shirt pocket. Greg's corpse slid into the hole and landed with a thud. Without waiting to be told, I dragged the heavy concrete lid back into place. It, too, landed with a thud.

"Use the sand and weeds you scraped off before to cover it all up. Make it fast, we need to go."

I glanced up and saw that Frank had been staring at his phone.

"You have radar on there?"

"Now!"

With the flat-headed log, I pushed the sand and vegetation back into place over the crypt. It looked like hell, but then so did the entire island.

"Grab the bags and let's go."

Carrying the bags was excruciating. Frank, of course, was ten feet back and had never lowered the gun. I wasn't just exhausted—my struggle with the duffel bags confirmed how weak I was. I might have a knife, but I wasn't sure I could take the old bastard if I got hold of him.

But if I got the chance, I'd try. That was for damn sure.

25

WITH THE EIGHT DUFFEL BAGS OF CASH NOW in the plane, Frank climbed aboard and I set out to pull the anchors that had kept Betty in place on the beach. She was already facing into the wind, aimed straight out from the shore into the waterless flat.

The wind was meaner than ever. A gust knocked me down and I landed on my left shoulder, hard. A stabbing pain tore across my collarbone.

I got onto my knees, pain slashing through my chest. Had I broken my clavicle?

Apparently not, because although the pain burning in my shoulder was excruciating, I managed to drag the port anchor back to the starboard hatch and drop it inside. But when I reached for the handles, pain shot through my left shoulder again.

Shit!

"Hurry it up, Reilly!"

I climbed aboard, sand blasting my back. Pain ripped at my neck as I reached for the hatch, changed hands and pulled it shut with my right hand. Everything I did to ready the plane for takeoff hurt like hell, and my teeth must have been clenched, because Frank noticed.

"What's wrong?" he said. "Looks like you're in pain."

Never expose weakness to your enemy.

"The storm's on full now. Doubt we'll make it."

Betty lifted onto one wheel and slammed back down. I grabbed the bulkhead wall—and yelped.

"Aagghh."

Fixed on mine, Frank's eyes narrowed.

"You need to sit up here with me for weight distribution," I said.

"Look at this." Frank held up his cell phone, open to a radar app. A swirling circle of yellow, orange, and red consumed the screen. Using his index finger and thumb, he zoomed in. Key West—in fact, all the Keys—could be seen directly in Irma's path, maybe a couple of hours away.

With that I got into the left seat, energized the batteries, and fired up the port engine. It coughed loudly.

Shit!

I'd forgotten about the damaged piston—it had gotten worse just before we landed.

"Come on, Betty. I love you, girl. Get us out of here."

The hundred feet of potential runway I'd seen semi-clearly earlier was now lost in sideways rain and what looked like static on an old black-and-white TV.

My shoulder hurt when I moved my left arm, and my right hand trembled as I checked the elevator with the wheel. What a way to freaking go. Wait—

"Hand me that first-aid kit under the instrument panel," I said.

"What for?"

"Now!"

I primed the starboard engine and engaged the starter—it kicked right on.

Frank leaned down with his right hand to grab the first-aid kit, the gun in his left hand aimed at my head. The knife I'd taken off Greg's corpse dug into my right side at an awkward angle. I wasn't sure I could reach it with my right hand, and my left arm was still screaming. Frank bent down to reach for the clasp on the kit—it would have been an excellent moment to make my move, if I *could* move—but he sat up quickly, the white box with the red cross on the lid in his hand. He placed it on his lap and popped open the lid.

"Hand me that bottle of Pepto Bismol," I said.

"You gonna puke?" He picked it up. The normally pink liquid inside was brown. "Don't look too good."

I spun the cap off and the familiar smell floated in the cabin. I drank deeply from my emergency supply of Pilar Rum.

"Liquid courage."

I took another swig, hesitated, and then handed Frank the bottle. He killed it.

Outside, the visibility was close to nil. I took hold of the throttles and stole a glance at Frank. There wasn't an ounce of fear on his face.

With the brake pulled tight, I ran up the RPMs until Betty was pulling hard at the bit, a racehorse ready to burst from the gate, trusting her jockey regardless of the situation.

I released the brake and she jumped forward, stumbling. When I pressed the throttles further, the tachometers redlined.

Betty picked up speed. We roared across the flats, zigged to port around a coral head, and zagged to starboard past a beached manatee—just a deranged killer and me.

A quick glance at our speed told me we needed twenty more knots. The starboard wheel hit a chunk of brain coral and the right wing lifted high, but I twisted the wheel and we evened out.

Water and whitecapped waves were visible ahead. If we hit the water with the landing gear down, the wheels would rip off and we'd nosedive.

Our speed was still shy and the water was coming fast. Betty fluttered on the brink, and I pulled back on the wheel just as the water met the plane. Betty jumped free of the flat and leaped into the air—briefly—then started to drop in a stall.

"No!"

The throttles were maxed so I edged the wheel forward and we surged toward the rushing water. A gust of wind caught us and we nearly went into a vertical climb that could cause another stall and nosedive.

I retracted the wheels and we skittered up a few hundred feet, gradually vectoring toward Key West. There was no choice but to fly into the wind.

The wings shook violently.

"Come on, Betty!"

Then the hurricane-smothered pre-dawn blackness swallowed us up. With nothing but instruments to guide me, I glanced at each one, otherwise unable to assess our position or altitude. I crabbed toward where I believed Key West to be.

CRASH!

Black feathers exploded on Betty's windshield. A crack formed in front of Frank and spider-webbed over toward me. I reduced power.

"What the hell?" Frank yelled.

"Cormorant. Protected species—"

He pointed to the glass a foot from his face. "You almost got lucky, Reilly."

Sparse lights flickered ahead. Slowly, familiar landmarks appeared in flashes, and I vectored east. Minutes passed at time and a half. Now I took us along the western perimeter of the island, still into the wind.

A flash of light—a flash of beach—Sunset Key and then blackness. A wall of buildings appeared, some with lights: Duval Street.

"Almost home, kid." Frank still held the gun but not aimed at me.

I tried my left arm. The pain wasn't as bad. Maybe my collarbone wasn't broken.

I added flaps and the altimeter spun backward, now at five hundred feet. My rain jacket was wedged under my leg and pulled tight against my hips. I'd relocated the knife into the waistband of my pants on my right side when I pulled the anchors. No way to reach it now.

Crap.

We flew past the La Concha, then east. Betty bounced up and down spanning a hundred feet of altitude as winds buffeted us. When we dropped suddenly, I added throttle, added flaps, and pulled back on the wheel. The wind counterpunched, and I again corrected our course dead into the wind.

"The airport's that way." Frank pointed to the left. "Where you going?"

"We need to keep the wind at our backs, go past the island, then turn back sharp into the wind and tack our way toward the airport."

I glanced down. The streets of Key West were full of water.

Jade.

I added throttle. We roared over Louie's Backyard—the rear deck was in tatters, and waves slammed over the patio. I held course out over the roiling waters—

WHOOSH!

A gust lifted us, high and fast. I reduced throttle—

GRRRIIINNNNNDDDDD!

The port engine's RPMs dropped and Betty jerked hard left. She angled hard toward the port deck. I kicked hard right rudder to stop the yaw. If we got too slow Betty would yaw left uncontrollably, resulting in a roll left nosedive. I added more to the starboard engine—

GRRRIIINNNNNDDDDD!

The screech from the port engine continued. The ninth-cylinder piston had to be coming apart—

"Come on, Betty! One more minute!"

"What's happening?"

I couldn't see the engine, but I suddenly remembered Ray saying the engine could catch fire and might explode if the piston blew.

"Blown piston!"

GRRRIIINNNNNDDDDD!

I stomped on the starboard rudder pedal, lowered the nose and aimed toward the runway at speed—

GRRRIIINNNNNDDDDD—

And pulled back on the port throttle. Smathers Beach flashed below us. Power dropped.

Betty pulled hard to port. The wind speed didn't drop—yaw increased—and we slid partially sideways. I crabbed Betty back and forth as we descended—condos below, mangroves—

"I see the runway!" Frank said.

The wind gusts shook us and I calculated the glide slope. Betty was too heavy for a single engine at slow speed.

"What's happening?"

"The port engine's dead—"

"We gonna make it?"

"If there's a break in the wind we'll drop like a rock."

Frank sat back, glanced at his treasure bags, and cinched his waist belt tighter. I hunched forward, my hands locked in a death clutch on the wheel, my leg aching from pressing the rudder so hard, attempting to keep Betty straight.

I clicked the microphone five times, which activated the runway approach lights. A faint blue glow appeared below us. The wheel was pressed forward, swirl of wind—there was the runway!

Tree branches were across the western end of the runway. Water blurred the asphalt—how deep was it?

Our angle of attack was sharp. One engine wasn't enough—twenty feet. I pulled back the wheel, final flap, reduced power—I lowered the wheels at the last second—

THUD!

We bounced to the starboard side close to the end of the runway. The water was shallow, inches—

THUD—

Reduced power, nose forward.

Betty stuck. Our speed dropped.

Frank smiled. "Damn, boy. Nice flying."

I added power to get Betty to the hangar by the private aviation terminal, where I could tie her down.

"I'm not saying anything about Greg Holmes, Frank. His boat will wash away in the storm and nobody will find that bunker. Haven't in thirty years." I glanced at him again. His eyes were calculating odds, risks. "And you're right I don't want the world to know the truth about my father. The money's yours. Just let me and Jade be."

He didn't respond. I stopped Betty in the same location we'd departed from last night. A glance at my Submariner and I was surprised to see it was 7:25 in the morning. Hurricane Irma's eye was nearly upon us.

The starboard engine hadn't even shut down yet when Frank yanked off his seat belt. "Let's get out of here," he said.

"Soon as I tie Betty down."

"No time, Reilly. Jade may already be under water. You want to save her or your plane?"

Frank's smile belied his mock concern.

SECTION 4

KEY WEST SATURDAY NIGHT

26

A1A WAS UNDER WATER. I DROVE THE ROVER along the dirt road that runs parallel to the highway. Boats littered the road.

The back of the Rover was loaded with the L.L. Bean bags. I'd done the math while schlepping the bags from the bunker to the plane, and based on the matching numbers that had been sketched on the wall of the tunnel and the bunker, there was over two million dollars in total.

The Rover shook in the wind, guided by a single headlamp. The other had been shattered when Frank forced me to crash through the gate at the private aviation terminal so I could drive onto the tarmac to retrieve the bags. At least I was able to tie Betty down while he unloaded the money. The port engine cowling was scorched and there was a hole the size of a coffee mug through the side where the piston must have exploded. Miracle we hadn't crashed.

The driver's-side windshield wiper didn't help one bit with the blinding rain. I turned onto Bertha and water surged past us. Trees were down everywhere, and the eye hadn't even hit yet. Nearly every storefront was covered with plywood. A tree blocked First Street past Advanced Auto. I drove over the curb and turned left down Flagler. A "for sale" sign blew past us, accompanied by coconuts and palm fronds.

How did my father become an undersecretary of state while his former smuggling associate rotted in jail? And his partner was killed in Medellín? Nothing I'd learned so far had shed any light on that.

I thought of Jade and pressed harder on the accelerator. Going faster was all but impossible. Waves flew up on each side of the Rover as we moved forward through flooded streets. A gray trash can bounced down the road and sailed toward us. I slammed on the brakes.

CRACK!

It caught the left fender, caromed off, spun, and sailed on.

"It ruins you, Reilly. You think I want to work in that freaking Butterfly Farm? All those pinhead faggots worrying over every damn chrysalis? Old losers and dumb-ass tourists oohing and aweing over insects like they was bars of gold. Torture, I'm telling you."

Frank's sudden diarrhea of the mouth was typical of someone who had escaped death. Or maybe it was caused by guilt about killing Greg. While I could never forgive the violence, the greed I understood. But I could never fully calculate how twenty years in prison might change a man for better or worse. Especially when his former partners had vanished along with the proceeds of doing what put you in prison in the first place. No way I'd cut Frank any slack, but I could see how a person could snap. That month on Tortola broke me, that's for damn sure.

Some homes had lost portions of their roofs. Siding had peeled off others. Trash was everywhere. Floodwaters rolled, buildings were boarded up as if the whole town had gone bankrupt, trees were down everywhere—many already stripped of leaves and branches—and there wasn't a soul in sight. Duval Street was a ghost town.

Thank God most people had obeyed the evacuation order. Had I, Greg would still be alive, and Jade—

I sped up, but the Rover hydroplaned, so I slowed down again.

Frank had a vacant smile on his face—imagining how to spend his newfound wealth? The victor coming home. How would Eleanor respond? No concern for Jade?

I slowed to turn at Angela Street, but a boat on a trailer was on its side blocking the road. We continued up to Fleming and drove through the intersection without stopping—something I did with every intersection, for that matter. No other cars were in sight.

Elizabeth Street was blocked by a downed tree, and we were finally able to turn right onto William Street. A couple of blocks before

Solares Hill, we came upon a house with a massive mahogany tree that had fallen onto it, dead center. I slowed and we both stared open-mouthed at the destruction. The house was split in half.

"That was the writer Shel Silverstein's house." Frank laughed. "He wrote a book I read maybe twenty times in prison called *The Giving Tree*."

"Ironic."

I stomped on the gas and turned onto Angela. Eleanor's house was just ahead. Water rushed down Elizabeth like a Disney flume ride and collided with a steady stream off Angela.

Jade.

I slammed the Rover into the curb, killed the engine, and ran from the vehicle toward the side of Eleanor's house.

I heard Frank's door slam behind me, and if he yelled for me to stop I didn't hear it above the shriek of the wind. Shutters shook, branches cracked, trees leaned over. A chunk of roofing from the neighbor's house was on the ground and I jumped over it.

The velocity of rain stung my cheeks and blurred my vision. At the side of the house I glanced back and saw Frank climbing the stairs toward Eleanor's front door. I dropped to my knees with a splash. With no flashlight, I crawled under the house, concrete and gravel ripping at my knees, until I reached the concrete lip and tunnel entrance. The lid was open, water pouring in from all sides.

"Jade!"

It was pitch-black inside.

"Jade?"

I dangled my legs inside the hole and dropped into the blackness. When my feet touched the top bale, I slipped.

"Jade!" I yelled at the top of my voice.

My gut was twisted torque-tight. There was literally no light. I couldn't see my hand in front of my face. I didn't want to jump on top of her, so I lowered myself slowly into water, a foot or more at the bottom.

I crouched and moved forward, waving my hands through the water. The tunnel was only four feet wide, so I spread my arms toward the sides and on my knees crawled forward through the tropically warm water into the blackness, feeling around as I went.

"Jade!"

Five feet—nothing. Ten feet—a lump!

I grabbed it—large and solid, an old bale of grass. Bottles rattled. The case of booze was on top of the bales and still above water.

Dammit!

Five more feet—nothing. Ten more—nothing!

My hands hit the end wall. I turned around.

The tunnel was empty.

What the hell? Had she escaped?

The Thompson.

I continued forward along the right side and felt the ground as I crawled. Water kept pouring in—it was getting deeper, maybe six inches more since I'd climbed in.

No sign of the Thompson, either.

What the hell?

I heard footsteps—someone was coming. Frank! He'd freak when he found Jade gone.

I took the knife from my belt and crouched next to the old bale.

All right, Frank, come and get me.

27

"FIND HER, REILLY?" FRANK SAID.

I stared up at the illuminated square hole where water rushed in from above and a faint silhouette hovered above it all.

"Come on down, Frank. Check it out."

I held the knife tightly under the water.

He shone the light down inside. I shielded my eyes but saw that water was indeed filling the cavern quickly.

"That's interesting, Reilly, 'cause I found something, too." He laughed.

Another black silhouette appeared over the entrance, and the water diverted as someone put their hands on the side—

Jade!

Frank laughed again.

"I'm sorry, Buck," Jade said.

What?

"Your old man used me, Reilly. Then never paid me."

"What the hell! *I* never used you. I never even knew my old man was a freaking dope smuggler—"

"I'm not blaming you, Reilly," Frank said. "I'm just settling the score."

"Jade, what are *you* doing?"

She just stared at me.

The sound of water pouring in and the light refracted off the ceiling boards that illuminated the dappled water inside the tunnel lit a flame of claustrophobia inside me. I rushed toward the opening—

BOOM!

The report from Frank's gun was magnified inside the flooded tunnel.

"Stop right there, Reilly. Next shot goes through your thick skull."

"The hell're you guys doing?"

"No traces, like I told you."

"What you *told* me was why you didn't need to kill me. It was true."

"Enough talk. Back up—all the way to the end of the cave. Now!"

I took tentative steps backward and shoved the knife back inside my pants as I went. Frank peeked down and aimed the light at me. I could hear a hushed discussion between him and Jade.

Legs dropped over the side of the entrance, followed by the light. Jade slowly lowered herself onto the bale. She was dry and her hair was up. She had on different clothes from last night. She hadn't been trapped in here at all.

"What's going on, Jade? What are you doing?"

Frank's legs dropped over the side—he, too, had a flashlight.

"Eleanor raised me, Buck. And Frank supported her from jail—"

"They're divorced."

"We tricked your ass, boy," Frank said.

"Divorced, yes, but for all her nastiness, Eleanor always wanted her cut."

"The storm was the perfect leverage," Frank said. "Beautiful Jade would drown if you didn't take me out to the bunker."

"Your father hid all our money from us," Jade said. "We were broke."

Frank jumped from the top bale into the water. A huge splash followed, but he landed surefooted and with his gun aimed at me.

"People love to put down ex-cons, Reilly," he said. "Their wives and the daughters of their murdered ex-partners, too. Life's been a bitch for us."

Frank reached over and pulled Jade closer to him. His hand slid down across her rear end.

"Get your hand off me!"

He howled with laughter. "Soon it'll be just you and me, Jadey."

Water continued to pour down around them. The level was now at least two feet deep, up a foot since I'd first entered the tunnel.

"You'll be an accessory to murder, Jade," I said.

"Where's the rope?" she said.

"I got your rope right here." He grabbed his crotch.

"Eleanor'll kick your ass you don't quit that shit—"

"Hell with that dried-up old hag," he said. "I feel young again."

The old bastard produced a long rope and handed it to Jade. I had to turn the tables. Fast.

"So you and Frank are an item, huh, Jade?"

"Shut up, Buck."

"Never saw that coming. December-April romance, to say the least."

"Nothing Viagra don't fix." Frank ran his hand down across Jade's breasts from behind her.

Jade pushed it away. "Cut the shit, Frank!"

"Then tie his ass up!" His voice had turned from butter to acid. "You said once we found the treasure we'd celebrate the way I wanted to, dammit."

She pulled the rope out of his hands and turned to face me.

"Turn around, Buck."

"You want to be an accessory to murder, Jade?"

"You won't drown down here—"

"Just what do you think that stuff pouring in here is? You hear Frank say 'no trace'? He's going to kill me, just like he murdered Greg Holmes out on Woman Key. He was a friend of mine."

She stood perfectly still, her eyes locked on mine.

"Turn around and face the wall, Reilly!"

"In cold blood like he was a mosquito," I said. "You don't think he'll kill me?"

Frank rushed forward a couple of steps, the gun thrust toward me. I bent down, my right hand reaching slowly behind my back for the knife.

"You don't shut up I'll kill you right now—no matter what Jade promised she'd do to me if I let you live."

Jade closed her eyes for a moment.

"What she'll do, huh, Frank? Maybe give you a nice sloppy blow-job like the boys in prison used to—"

"Shut up!"

"He'll kill you, too, Jade, you don't give him what he wants. He killed his daddy with a baseball bat—"

BOOM!

Another deafening gunshot. But this one went through the tree roots that had grown through and damaged the ceiling of the tunnel. Dirt fell in a clump, and water started to pour in through the middle of the roots.

"Turn around. Not another word."

I spun around and put my hands against the wall. Jade came up behind me.

"I'm sorry, Buck." Her voice was a whisper.

"He's crazy. Don't do this—"

"Hey—what are you two whispering about?"

She took my left arm and pulled it behind my back. She slipped the rope over my hand. It had a slipknot on the end.

"You know he's crazy, Jade."

"Are you conspiring against me?" Frank said.

Jade whipped around. "Shut up, Frank! Just shut the hell up and let me do this."

"Don't tell me to shut up, bitch," Frank said. "You do what I tell you, you know what's good for you."

Her grip tightened on my forearm and then pushed free—*WHAP!*

Frank took a couple of quick steps back, the hand holding the flashlight now up on his cheek. She'd slapped him.

"Don't ever touch me again, Frank," she said. "No slaps, no gropes, and nothing else. You can buy all the whores you want with your half of the mon—"

He rushed forward—*CRACK!*

Frank hit her with a jab. She slumped forward but caught hold of my belt to keep from falling.

"Now tie his ass up."

Jade's hands shook as she tightened the rope on my left wrist. The pain in my shoulder screamed. Then she wrapped the rope around my other wrist and tied it off.

"Wrap it around his legs."

Water continued to pour down, and the wind howled outside the tunnel entry. The eye of the hurricane had to be close. The flow from the ceiling had quadrupled. As the storm surge increased, the water would come faster and harder.

Based on the increased water flow, the tunnel would be full in ten minutes max.

My legs were now bound.

"There, happy?" she said.

"Turn around, you little bitch."

"What are you—"

"You're a lying little tramp. Turn around."

"No, Frank—"

"I did twenty freaking years, goddammit, while you were living here on the island, lying on the beach, sporting that tight little body in strip clubs—"

"Frank, please, I'll do whatever you want—"

"Shut up!"

The water splashed behind me—he must have spun her around and shoved her against my back. He ran the rope around my waist and then hers, cinched it tight, and tied her hands behind her back. I felt his hand reach down to her crotch, linger, rubbing. She whimpered, her head falling forward against my shoulder. Then she twisted.

"Stop it, you sick asshole!"

He pushed her—us—and I slammed face first into the brick wall. Did it give a little or was that my nose crumpling? The taste of blood was my answer.

Frank finished wrapping the rope around our legs and tied the end off on Jade's arm.

"You deserve each other," Frank said. "For eternity."

Jade's whimper echoed in the small chamber that would become our crypt.

Frank sloshed back through the tunnel, and when he got to the end he trained the light back on us. The water was now up to my waist, which would be higher on Jade.

"This is for you, Crazy Charlie, Tommy. Paybacks are hell."

With that Frank climbed up the bale and out of the hole.

SLAM!

He'd closed the hatch.

28

THE WATER NOW CAME ONLY FROM THE HOLE in the ceiling. Thank God—

BOOM! BOOM! BOOM! BOOM! Click.

Frank had emptied the .357 Magnum into the lid. Once again there was the sound of water as it rushed through the perforations into our black chamber. It was the only sound other than Jade's hysterical shout.

"Rot in hell, Frank!"

"Jade—"

"That son of a bitch! I can't believe he'd—Eleanor will kill him!"

"Jade—"

"I'll kill him myself—"

"Listen to me, dammit!"

I couldn't see her but she became still against me. The water poured in like a fire hose with the spigot opened full.

"You double-crossed me," I said.

"I've known you a few days. You need to understand that Eleanor was the closest thing to a relative I had. Yeah, Frank is whacked, but we're some kind of dysfunctional survivors."

A burst of wind rattled above us—something slapped us on the sides of our heads.

"The hell?" Jade said.

Water now splashed down on us with greater force. The amount had increased—again.

"We're running out of time," she said.

"I have a knife in the back of my pants," I said. "Hold still. I'll try to reach it."

With a twisting motion to create space between our bodies, I dragged my bound hands over the belt loops of my pants. The knife handle dug into the small of my back.

"The water's up to my chest!"

I bent my knees—

"You're dragging me under!" she said.

Gales of wind roared outside, now louder from the open hole above our heads.

WHAP!

Again something slapped my head. I twisted to reach the knife—tree roots whipped around the ceiling of the chamber and then slapped against the water.

"The big mahogany must be blowing around," I said.

Another blast of air and the gap in the ceiling grew wider. Dirt poured in.

"Can you reach your knife?"

My fingers scraped along the top of my pants. My arm was at an awkward angle, but I felt the rough-hewn wood handle. *Careful not to push...* The knife slipped down into my underwear.

"Don't move," I said.

"Hurry up, Buck!

CRASH!

The lightning strike flashed inside the tunnel from the now foot-wide hole.

My fingers cramped up, bent at each knuckle.

"Aaggh!"

"Do you have it?"

I forced my hand to close around the handle against the cramp—three fingers and my thumb had a tenuous grip on the end of the handle.

"Hang on while I stand taller to pull it out."

"Hurry!"

With a fragile grip, I lifted the knife higher and pulled it free.

A wind gust roared past. The roots swung wildly, dirt tumbling in, and the hole grew bigger.

"The tree's falling!" Jade cried. "It'll crush us!"

Cramps tore at my fingers, but I had a death grip on the knife's handle.

I sawed at the rope against my leg—

"Don't stab me," Jade said.

I sawed in short bursts. The pain was too great to do it all at once. No surprise that the knife was razor-sharp—Greg was fastidious about his equipment. I felt the rope fray—

KABOOM!

Whether it was more lightning or another blast from Irma, the mahogany roots slapped down and forced us against the brick wall. Water flooded down in a torrent.

"Bu—ck!"

Jade choked—she was nearly under.

I dug at the rope like it was a snake trying to strangle me—

Snap!

The rope broke free, and instantly there was room between us.

"Turn around!" I said.

A loud cough was all I heard.

I bent my knees until I was up to my nose in water, leaned back, grabbed Jade by the crotch, and stood tall. She lifted up.

"God ... help me!"

"Turn around. I'll cut the ropes on your hand."

"I'll drown if ... I—"

"I'm going to drop you—"

"No!"

"Bend your knees, and when you hit the bottom, jump and spin to face away from me. I'll catch you!"

"No!"

"Do it!"

I pulled my hand out from under her and she sank.

C'mon!

I felt her turn. She launched up and crashed into my back. I extended my fingers—her hands brushed them—I grabbed her wrist!

"Stop kicking!" I said. "I'll lean forward. Be still while I cut the rope."

I leaned over until my face was in the water and sawed away at her hand and the rope against her arm. She might have screamed—maybe I cut a gash in her hand. I lifted my head, sucked in a breath, and went back under.

Saw... saw ... saw ...

Snap—her wrists were free!

She pushed off me and vanished.

"Jade? Jade!"

I twisted around. She was clutched onto the case of Prohibition-era booze like it was a life ring.

"Take the knife and cut my wrists free."

She looked upward—the hole was now a foot and a half across. The mahogany had indeed toppled, the root system weak because of the tunnel below. We could have been crushed.

"I can fit through," Jade said.

"Cut me loose and we'll go."

"I don't want to drown."

I bit my lip. *Keep calm. Don't freak her out.*

"Jade, cut me loose. I don't want to drown either."

"I can't see your hands ... The knife ... I don't want—"

"I'm going to turn around, Jade. The knife is in my hands. It's sharp. It'll cut through fast and we'll get out—*Jade*!"

She shook her head and her eyes cleared, just enough.

"Take the knife from my hands and cut me loose. Then I'll boost you out the hole."

I didn't wait. I spun around fast and leaned forward. She'd already betrayed me once. Would she do it again? Would she leave me to die?

One ... two ... three ...

She took hold of my arms, slid her hands down, and grabbed the knife.

Four ... five ... six ...

Saw ... saw ... saw ...

God, please …

Saw … saw …

Snap.

The rope fell free and I spun around and grabbed her. I held her above the water level—almost to the ceiling. My neck was bent as I struggled through the mahogany roots toward the hole. I hoisted Jade up like an Olympic power lifter.

She clawed at the side of the hole and dirt rained down—*CLUNK.* Asphalt, too. The road must have given way next to the tree.

My mouth was under water. I leaned back, but the water splashed around as she kicked—I couldn't scream for her to stop.

On my tiptoes, I pushed my head sideways against the ceiling. As I caught a breath, she grabbed hold of a root above the surface. I shoved her ass upward—

She lifted free from my hands. She was up!

Using the roots, I pulled myself forward and caromed into the case of booze now afloat—it popped open. I yanked a bottle out and used it to gouge the sides of the hole—far too narrow for my shoulders.

My head was halfway out. I sucked in rain, wind and dirt.

Jade knelt down and screamed something into the hole, but the shriek of the wind erased hers.

She pivoted, glanced back at me with sad eyes, and ran toward Eleanor's house.

"No! Jade—no!"

29

MY HEAD WAS HALFWAY UP THE HOLE. I HUNG ON TO THE ROOTS with one hand and used the bottle to scrape at the dirt with the other. Water rose around me. It would soon cover my face.

Seconds—all I had were seconds.

An image of my parents at the farm in Middleburg—laughing—flashed into my mind's eye. Mom looked pissed. Shark Beach—

Sharks were all around us. Ben and I were in the water—

One grabbed my leg!

It pulled!

I was dragged under—

Into the black water. I felt a hand—it pulled at me.

My mind snapped back to the moment. I saw the hand disappear under the tree roots. The blackness was almost total, but the hand had been white.

I kicked off the side wall down toward the floor—roots dug at my back—and clawed along the bottom. I was about to go up for air when the hand grabbed my arm and pulled me forward.

I felt burlap—the old bale of dope. Then a flash of Jade's face—she'd come back!

I kicked off from the bottom and climbed toward the hatch.

My hands flailed as oxygen deprivation burned—I caught something solid. Jade's hand. It pulled me into a tunnel of light, and we popped up on the other side of the tree. I caught a breath in the tunnel opening.

"C'mon, Buck, hold on."

Panting deeply, I hung tight on Jade's arm with my one operable hand. When my feet hit the bale, I shuffled them until they caught and I kicked myself upward. When my arms caught the sides of the hatch, I wrapped them around it.

"Good God," she said.

My breathing was so hard that stars danced in my eyes. I glanced up at her.

"Thought … you'd left me … to drown."

Her face twisted into a scowl. "Told you I was going to open the hatch."

No point in saying I hadn't heard a word she'd said, thanks to being stuck in the hole, the roiling winds, and nearly drowning.

"You brought a souvenir?"

"What are you talking about?"

She nodded toward what for the past couple of minutes I'd considered my bad hand. My arms were still wrapped around the concrete lip of the hatch, but a bottle of Prohibition booze was tightly clutched between my fingers.

I started to laugh, but Jade held her index finger to her lips and pointed to the floorboards of Eleanor's house above us. How could they have not heard the mahogany tree fall? Would they know the tunnel was exposed?

With the strength I could gather, I pulled myself out of the concrete chute and rolled to the side into the flowing water. But I could breathe, so I lay there for a second gathering my strength.

Too bad I couldn't kick in Eleanor's door, find Frank, and strangle the life out of him. But in addition to his .357 Magnum, he must have the Thompson submachine gun, since it hadn't been in the tunnel.

"Friend, or foe?" I said when I'd closed the hatch and snapped the latch closed.

"I'm sorry, Buck."

We held a long glance.

"History," I said.

"What?"

"You and Frank have history. You and I don't."

"Frank's gotten a *lot* crazier, Buck. I didn't know—you have to believe me!"

Didn't matter. Brushes with death, nearly crashing Betty, the hurricane, drowning—maybe they'd made me pragmatic. But then, pragmatism was not what I needed right now. I needed to be a psychotic killer. One who could withstand a hail of machine-gun fire long enough to strangle the son of a bitch who'd already tried and would certainly try again to kill us.

"We need to get out of here," Jade said. "Quietly."

After a three-count, I rolled onto my knees. The gravel that dug into them sharpened my senses. Jade led the way toward the opening in the lattice. She hesitated at the end and faced me.

"What's the plan?"

The reality that the end of the short tunnel had been bricked up had gnawed at me since we'd first found it. My gut told me what that meant, and if we didn't act now, Frank might come to the same conclusion. That greedy bastard wouldn't settle for the couple million we'd recovered on Woman Key. He'd want every penny he could find.

"Future furniture," I said.

Her eyes narrowed. "What about it?"

"Let's go to my father's house," I said. "There must be a second half to the tunnel."

Her eyes grew wide. "If that's true, won't it be flooded?"

"Only one way to find out."

She glanced down at the bottle in my hand. "So you *do* want a souvenir?"

I shook my head. "I'm thirsty."

Her brow furrowed, and she turned and crawled away.

"Jade?"

She glanced back.

"Thanks for saving my life."

A warmth softened her features, and for the first time I felt as if I'd seen her with her guard down. It only lasted an instant, but in that brief window I saw her in a new light that made her attractive.

She crawled forward and I kept close. I didn't trust her enough to feel comfortable having her out of my sight.

30

MORNING HAD COME AND THE LIGHT WAS YELLOW. We were at the corner of Eleanor's house. The wind and rain roared past so fast it blurred my vision. Loose matter, branches, trash, anything not battened down flew over and around us at a velocity that would take our heads off if some of it hit us. We needed to get under cover or we'd get killed. A full-force hurricane had hit the Keys.

Jade tugged at my arm. I nodded toward the vacant house across the street.

Just then a two-by-four shot over our heads and into a palm tree—slit it clean in half and kept going. We had to move.

I grabbed Jade's hand and we took off at a sprint. Once we were beyond the cover of Eleanor's house, the wind knocked us hard off course—our legs tangled and we tumbled into the floodwaters devouring Angela Street. I spun, and Jade fell on top of me. My left collarbone again screamed in pain. An orange five-gallon paint bucket skidded past our heads.

We crawled toward the far side of the street. Water sloshed under my feet, maybe six inches deep—what would it be elsewhere? Had the eye already passed? Had the calm that came with it passed by while we were fighting for our lives in the tunnel?

Leaves slapped and bit like bee stings on my face and arms, and branches hurt like hell. Across the road I managed to make it up the side yard to behind the lee of the house. Jade crashed into me and grabbed hold like I was her long lost brother.

My father's former house was boarded tight with plywood, not the more common fancy aluminum shutters. Like Eleanor's, it was elevated on piers to provide clearance against floodwaters. If there was a tunnel here, it would probably be accessed from underneath the house or somewhere in the yard.

Hunched over, I continued through the narrow passageway between the house and the white-board fence, which was shaking. The path was gravel with concrete pavers, any of which could be a hatch to a tunnel, but there was nothing obvious.

There was a gate that prevented access to the backyard. It was secured with a rusted Master lock. Crap. I pushed hard against the gate, but it didn't budge.

"Now what?" Jade screamed above the screech of the wind.

I shoved the bottle of booze into my jacket pocket, bent down, interlocked my fingers, and glanced up at Jade. Game, she placed her hand on my shoulder, and when she jumped I lifted her up until she was on top of the gate. Then she straddled it and disappeared on the other side.

It was too high for me to pull myself up. There was nothing in the narrow side yard I could use except—

I knelt and dug my fingers through the pea gravel around the edge of a concrete paver. Already raw, my fingertips smeared blood on the paver. I dug under the corner and was finally able to pull it up to a sucking sound as the wet earth released it. After two vicious slams of the paver onto the lock, the clasp broke free.

Rain needled my face with the force of a manic acupuncturist. I kicked the gate open to find a small plunge pool, a charcoal grill, and potted plants stripped of leaves. No sign of Jade.

"Jade!" Nothing. "Jade?"

"Over here." Her voice came from the other side of the house.

A huge dirt devil full of leaves, an orange dinosaur toy, and the life ring from the pool spun around the backyard like a sentry. I had to duck past the dinosaur.

Jade was on the opposite side of the house, on her knees, pulling at a small shrub. Blackness behind it indicated it could be a way under the house. I bent next to her and grabbed the other side of the bush. We pulled hard and the roots let go. I tossed it to the side.

"Do you still have a flashlight?" I said.

"No."

Everything outside was storm-soaked. From my knees I peered under the house. On the corner toward the back was a large square. I walked around to the back corner and found that it was a small plastic storage shed. Inside were several small tools, cans of paint, drop cloths, a bag of charcoal, and a lighter.

Bingo.

I grabbed a handful of items, got back up to where Jade waited, and crawled under the house. She followed. With my collection of scrounged items dumped in front of us, I handed her a toilet plunger.

"What the hell?"

I tore off a section of the drop cloth, wrapped it around the handle of the plunger, and tied it off.

"What the hell are you doing?"

"Making a torch."

From my pocket I removed the Prohibition bottle of booze. Using the butt of the garden trowel, I shoved the cork down into the hole—rum splashed out. She held the plunger up.

"First things first," I said.

I sniffed the ninety-plus-year-old booze. It smelled amazing.

It tasted even better.

I handed the bottle to Jade, who took a swig. Her face curled for a moment.

"That is damn good."

"Cuba's finest."

I hated to waste it but poured booze all over the fabric on the plunger and grabbed the lighter.

"Don't burn the house down," Jade said.

"Hold it low."

With a flick of the lighter, the booze-soaked torch lit right up. She held it away from us toward the front of the house.

"Let's go," I said.

31

THERE WAS NO CONCRETE ENTRY HATCH like there'd been under Eleanor's house. Nor was there an enclosed shaft that could lead from the house to a tunnel.

"The mark on my map had a small *X* where we found the hatch," I said. "The note on top of the map also said 'Close to future furniture.'"

"The old mahogany was on the far corner of the property." She pointed to the other end of the house from where we were kneeling.

The flame on the torch was fading. I retrieved the bottle of booze, took another swig—it burned—and dumped the rest onto the torch. The flame leaped toward the floorboards of the house above us. We went down to the corner of the house.

"There's nothing here, Buck."

Damn.

I began stabbing at the top of the dirt with the garden trowel. The blade went about an inch below the surface. I stabbed the ground repeatedly in a grid pattern, three feet by three feet. After a dozen attempts I hit something hard—*CLUNK*. Jade and I exchanged a glance.

I stabbed the trowel down with renewed vigor.

CLUNK!

The topsoil was moist and scraped away easily.

"What if it's just the sewer line? Or the water line?" Jade said.

"Be positive, will you?"

I kept scraping, and after several sweeping drags of the trowel, a flat, hard surface appeared. A two-foot square. No hinge or handle.

"Hold the torch closer."

I dug down on the corner closest to us. After two inches, the concrete recessed an inch inward. I continued around the sides of the square.

"It's a lid."

Once two sides were exposed, I jammed the tip of the trowel up under the lid and pushed down.

Nothing.

I changed my position, held the trowel with both hands, placed a rock underneath it to improve the angle, and pressed all my weight against it.

The handle started to bend—the lid lifted!

I cleared away the rest of the dirt around the perimeter, then stood above it. "Help me," I said.

We grasped two sides and pulled upward—the concrete lid opened! We slid the concrete lid off the shaft and dropped it. There was a black hole below. Jade lowered the torch into it. There were the same types of wood walls as we'd found in the tunnel across the street. We could see a few crates below.

I sat on the edge. Outside, the storm raged with the wrath of Dante's Inferno. According to my Submariner it was 9:15 a.m. Right when the eye was supposed to hit.

I lowered myself into the hole and dropped.

THUD.

My feet landed on solid ground with only a slight splash. Jade handed me the torch. At the end of the room was a bricked-up wall. Had to be the opposite side of the same tunnel, split in two. One side for each of our fathers. Tommy's side held weed, guns, and money. What would we find in Dad's tunnel? There were no maps or numbers on the walls.

Water spewed out along the edges of the brick and squirted out in a narrow stream from the middle. The other side was full, and the pressure would be strong to topple the wall.

"Help!"

Jade hung from the entry behind me. I grabbed her with one arm and lowered her to the ground.

"Not sure how long that wall will hold," I said.

There were three metal footlockers and a couple more crates of booze, but no L.L. Bean duffel bags and no old bales of grass. We popped the tops off the footlockers and stood back to take inventory.

"More notebooks?" Jade said.

The footlockers contained six brown notebooks identical to those I'd already found. There was one plastic bin, which I popped open to find a gallon bag of white powder. Jade pulled open the seal, stuck her finger inside, and tasted it.

"Cocaine."

"No shit."

"Shit's right. No cash."

All of a sudden water began to push harder through new gaps on the edges of the brick wall.

"Grab the notebooks," I said.

"What the hell for?"

"Just do it!"

Jade scooped up the notebooks.

"Hey!" She looked up fast. "There's a cashbox underneath in the last crate." She unclasped the lid. It was full of cash, neatly stacked by denomination.

A brick broke free near the top of the wall. Water shot forward and hit Jade in the back.

"Let's go," I said.

She held the torch while I struggled to lift the cash box and notebooks up through the hatch. My arm shook and I felt the little strength I had left drain from my body—I was flashing back to throwing the L.L. Bean duffel bags out of the bunker on Woman Key. I refocused and reassessed the situation.

"I'm taking this, too." She clutched the plastic bag that bulged with coke.

"Whatever, let's roll—"

The top of the wall came free with a crash and water poured over the edge and into the tunnel. Jade leaned the torch against the wall below the hatch, which was also made of brick, held firmly to what must be a kilo of cocaine, and waited for me to give her a leg up.

"Jump when I lift you." She did and I lifted her into the opening, where she grabbed hold and shimmied out.

Water poured in and the mortar between the bricks down the center of the wall started to break off, creating additional streams of water.

My left shoulder screamed as I stacked two of the footlockers, but before I could get the third the wall broke apart. Water poured forward and knocked me off balance. I leaped atop a footlocker and jumped upward—the flood doused the flame on the torch—and I caught the edge of the hatch.

Jade grabbed my arms.

"Aaggh—my shoulder!"

A vision of being trapped in the last tunnel helped me push through the pain. In a flash I was up and out and kneeling on the ground, my entire body shaking uncontrollably. Jade was crawling toward where we'd gained entry under the house. At the edge, in the light, she popped open the cash box and fanned through the stacks while I caught my breath.

"Maybe another twenty grand here." The disappointment on her face made it hard to keep a serious face. "At most."

"Take it," I said. "The coke, too. I'll go through the notebooks and see if there's anything else of interest."

She handed them to me. "What are we going to do now?"

"Get the hell out of here before Frank shows up. He'll figure out pretty quickly that we escaped—then he'll see there was another section of tunnel and assume we found something valuable. He knows where we both live. We could go to a my friend Ray's—"

"I'm going home. I have plenty of options on this island."

Before I could protest, she said what was really on her mind.

"How do we get the money back from Frank?" Her eyes were cold and calculating.

"Let's meet up later," I said. "The La Concha. Say, one o'clock."

She nodded. "You going to be okay?"

"I'm fine. I just want to get home, clean up, eat, and figure out how to get all my money back."

With that, she crawled out from the house. The moment she stood, the wind knocked her sideways. She ran with the gust toward the back of the house. By the time I crawled out, she'd disappeared around the back. Out front, trees bent in the wind, but the water level was no higher in the road.

I caught a flash of Jade running down Angela toward Elizabeth with the wind at her back, and then she vanished into the mist. My Rover was parked one house down from Eleanor's. I hesitated. Frank would hear it start up. And so with the notebooks buried under my jacket, I fought my way into the storm. Popped the Rover's door open, put it in neutral, and with the help of the wind pushed it back away from Eleanor's.

The road was flat. I kept one hand on the wheel and pushed with the other in the open door so I could keep the vehicle straight. Four houses down I turned the wheel and backed the Rover into a driveway, jumped inside, started the engine, and turned in the opposite direction, toward the La Concha.

I'd be temporarily safe there, provided it hadn't crumpled, but judging by what I saw on the way, I figured the eye had hit farther north. Not that the carnage wasn't horrific—Hurricane Irma had made fast destruction of mature trees along with buildings and roofs that weren't sturdy and had doubtless destroyed an untold number of lives.

The trip back to the La Concha was slow. Wind mercilessly blew the boxy Rover around. I couldn't park at the hotel or Frank would find me. I turned on Fleming, then Bahama, and parked behind the retail buildings that faced Duval.

I was the only fool in the rain.

32

THE LA CONCHA WAS LIKE A BOMB SHELTER. People were huddled in the center of the open lobby with seat cushions and single mattresses dragged from guest rooms.

They looked up from their cover, all eyes wide at the sight of someone who'd come in from the storm. *Okay, I must look like a zombie fresh out of the grave, too.*

Questions began flying my way as I walked toward the stairs.

"What's it like out there?"

"How bad is the damage?"

I turned around to face the group. "There's flooding. Plenty of trees are down and some homes damaged."

Climbing six floors—in the dark, in my shape—was, to say the least, slow. The corridor that led to my corner suite was nearly black, the only light from an empty guest room in the middle of the hall with the door open. Lindy had probably opened doors on each floor to provide light to the darkened hallways.

My door swung open and I saw—again—that Frank had trashed my room. Prick.

I ground my teeth. It felt like a steam room. Who knew when the power would be restored and the air conditioning working again? From my window I could usually see down Duval Street all the way to the water in each direction, but the visibility now was a couple of blocks.

The storm was still howling, and outside it looked like a life-size game of pickup sticks.

The six new notebooks contained more names, with addresses, times of day, and more numbers. I wasn't sure what any of it meant. There were other maps of a larger scale with Latin names like Envigado, El Poblado and Rionegro.

There was a page with four phone numbers but no names.

More mysteries.

Between the two tunnels we'd found a machine gun, bales of marijuana, a few pounds of cocaine, Prohibition-era booze, forty thousand-plus in cash, and more notebooks. I pushed the notebooks away, wishing I'd never followed up on the ones I'd found at home. Trouble begets trouble begets trouble, like always.

I bit the bullet and collapsed onto my bed. I forced myself to get up after a power nap and began to put the mess of my suite back together again.

Noon came and went and the storm had passed to the northwest. There was no power on Key West, so there was no way to get an update without a radio—which made me question Betty's status. They eye hadn't hit Key West, but if Irma's winds had raked the coast, Betty was done for.

All I could think of beyond Betty's fate was to track Frank down, retrieve my father's money, and beat him to within an inch of his life. But how? He'd be expecting me. The logical place to start was back at Eleanor's. Would Frank still be there? Eleanor had said he lived in a trailer on Stock Island. There were hundreds of them, or at least there had been before Irma, so that would be like searching for a blade of grass in a field.

A pang of guilt cleared my mind. There was so much damage on-island, and probably worse up the Keys, that I knew I should help search for missing people or animals and lend a hand to start the restoration effort. But Frank had killed Greg Holmes. He'd tried to kill Jade and me, and my mouth watered at the thought of retribution. The son of a bitch.

And Betty's port engine had blown thanks to him.

I rubbed my closed eyes with the heels of my hands.

First things first. Betty's status had to outweigh my thirst for revenge. Jade was set to arrive here in ten minutes, so I loaded my backpack with items that could be handy in making our way around the island: a flashlight, duct tape, a roll of plastic, a small pair of bolt cutters, and the knife.

After a slow descent in the dark down the steps, I found the hotel lobby devoid of people. Everyone must have left to go assess their personal situations once the storm had passed. My watch read 1:05.

Jade was a few minutes late. I slumped into a comfortable chair and leaned back, and exhaustion overcame me.

Swirls of dark clouds came at me fast. Betty pitched and yawed into the wind, lighting bolts flashing ahead. A tornado with houses spinning inside it rolled off the starboard wing. A dark presence was close—behind me—next to me. A gun stabbed into my gut.

Frank, wearing an evil grin, his eyes blood-red—

"Buck!"

My eyes popped open. Lindy stood in front of me, shuffling his feet.

"Sorry for waking you up."

I glanced at my Submariner: 1:45.

"Did a woman come by looking for me?"

Lindy hesitated. "Not lately."

Damn. Could Frank have found her?

With no idea where she lived, there wasn't much I could do. Jade had said she had plenty of options on Key West. She wouldn't sit at home, where Frank could find her.

Lindy followed me toward the check-in counter.

"Any word on the damage?" I said.

"It's bad. We got a battery-operated radio in the kitchen, and US-1 Radio never stopped transmitting."

"Where'd the eye hit?"

"Cudjoe. Flattened it." Lindy winced. "Big Pine was hit hard, too."

What about the mustached bartender from the Green Parrott? Sudden nausea hit and I leaned against the counter. "Death toll?"

"Nothing certain, but rumor has it a couple dozen. We're all crazy for staying, but nobody seen a storm like this here before. Where you headed?"

"Check on my plane."

"Let me know what you see."

Lindy was pale and his hands shook as he rubbed sweat off his forehead.

"People in the Keys are strong," I said. "We'll bounce back."

"Keys strong. Yeah, I hope so, Buck."

With that I exited at the back of the hotel and found an inconceivable mess in the parking area. A large gumbo limbo from the neighboring property had fallen, torn the fence down, and crushed a few cars in the process, a convertible mustang's soft-top had been decapitated, and mopeds were piled in a heap. Every other inch of ground was littered with leaves, sticks, and rubbish. My Rover had a large branch leaning against it and was covered in organic matter. Again soaked with sweat after cleaning the Rover off, I began what became a serpentine journey through the battered streets toward the airport.

Power lines were down—which would prolong the recovery—and there was standing water everywhere. The trees that had not been blown over were stripped bare of their leaves, which were plastered all over everything in sight. At the end of Whitehead, roiling waves and wind slamming the ocean side of the southernmost marker had stripped off some of its red, black, and yellow paint. Seaweed and sand covered the road.

Angry waves pounded the shore, and lines of breaking white-fringed seas extended to the south as far as I could see. Nature had served up one ass-kicking storm. The palm trees that weren't stripped looked like fast-swimming squid, their palm fronds-cum-tentacles extended straight behind them.

Carnage. Everywhere.

And this wasn't even where the eye had hit. The trailer parks up the Keys were notorious for being hurricane bait, and if not properly anchored they might become trailer-size projectiles. Buffett was right when he said trailers were better off as beer cans. I couldn't imagine what the scene was like on Cudjoe and Big Pine.

I hopped out, turned the hubs on the Rover, and placed it in four-wheel high gear. Atlantic Boulevard was solid seaweed, over six inches of muck. There was a lone man with a shovel and wheelbarrow in front of the Atlantic House bed-and-breakfast. He'd already cleared a large swath, and he didn't look up at me as I passed slowly by. He personified the determination and strength it would take to overcome and rebuild.

Keys Strong.

Bertha Street was also a washout. A1A in front of Smathers beach was horrendous. The Rover slipped and slid through the soft mess that had lodged in the street. I navigated up onto the shoulder on the wrong side of the road, still unrecognizable but solid.

Three large sailboats had run aground on the beach. Some blocked the road and others had washed all the way to the other side of A1A and into the woods by the salt pond. I could see the masts of other sailboats above the dune by the beach. Ahead there was a twenty-foot powerboat in the middle of the road. What would be the status of the sailboats anchored out near Wisteria Island and Sunset Key?

My stomach churned. Frank had allowed me only a moment to secure Betty when we returned from Woman Key. What would I find at the airport?

I drove forward slowly and steered around the boats, larger mounds of sand, boulders of coral, sponges, trees, and an empty car upside down in the street.

At the airport I reentered the gate I'd smashed the Rover through under Frank's orders this morning and immediately hit the brakes. The runway was covered with water and debris. I put the Rover back in gear and headed for my plane. Every one I passed looked as if it had been sandblasted.

Betty?

A palm frond had wrapped around her fuselage The cowling on her port engine was smeared black and the windshield was cracked. The hole I'd spotted when we landed was the size of a fist. What if the piston had exploded downward toward the cockpit instead of out to the side? I might not be standing here. Or Frank might not be wherever he was now, sitting on his ass counting his money.

My father's money.

Drug money.

Betty's restoration, not yet completed, had taken a major step backward thanks to Irma. Good thing we hadn't had her painted yet. I popped the aft hatch.

"I'm sorry, old girl."

Greg Holmes was dead and buried in the bunker. How could I keep that quiet and live with myself? To protect my dear deceased drug-smuggling father's legacy?

Shit.

Key West Airport would become an important link to the Lower Keys' recovery effort. Betty was out of commission, but with the batteries clicked on she still had juice. I toggled on the radio and changed the frequency to Ray's and my preferred emergency channel.

"Key West calling Ray Floyd. I repeat, Key West calling Ray Floyd."

After three minutes of the same hail, the static was broken.

"Thank God, Buck! We thought you were a goner for sure. How's Betty?"

"You and Ron Weiner?"

"Nope. An old friend of yours showed up here at Spruce Creek. Scarlet Roberson."

"*What?*"

"You're still crazy, Buck Reilly." Scarlet's voice, in the background.

What the heck?

"And Betty?" Ray said.

"Long story, but she didn't much like flying during the hurricane—"

"You *left*? Where'd you go?"

Now was not the time for details. "Wasn't gone long and I'm back here on-island. She's in one piece, but cylinder nine blew. I was lucky I didn't get killed."

Ray informed me of how crazy I was and then filled me in on the news from Irma. Everything from Cudjoe to Islamorada had been thrashed, and the storm was now flooding Naples and Tampa.

"The road up the Keys is closed," Ray said. "Nobody's allowed in or out."

Frank couldn't escape. I smiled.

"And it's about time you called, Buck. Irma's headed north, so we need to get the hell out before the storm hits here."

"Where are you headed? And what do you mean 'we'?"

"I'm coming down to help," Scarlet said.

"That's crazy. The airport's closed and the runway here's a mess."

"I work there, remember?" Ray said. "Better start cleaning up that runway because we're heading that way—"

"Are you crazy?"

"It's not much, but we have supplies from the Red Cross," Scarlet said. "Fifty cases of water."

The tone in her voice caused me to smile. It had been a long time since I'd heard that insistent intonation. Hell, it had been years since I'd spoken to her at all. Truth be told, I wanted Ray to get the Beast back here as soon as possible. I had plans for her.

33

THE AIRPORT HAD A FRONT-END LOADER locked in the yard past U.S. Customs and the FedEx office. I used a stand-up ashtray to break off the padlock—Irma had honed my skills at breaking and entering. Since nobody was in sight, I should be able to clear the runway and not get arrested. The bright yellow Caterpillar 906M stood right out, but the keys weren't in the ignition.

It didn't take long to find the red battery and brown starter wires. I cut the battery wires and spliced the two together. I then cut the brown starter wire—

Zap.

The knife flew out of my hand!

Damn! The battery had shocked me.

After I shook my hand a few times, I touched the ends of the two brown wires together—

VRROOOMMM.

The Cat started up.

For once a good deed needed to go unpunished. The sooner the runway was cleared the better. A foot of standing water contained by sand and mud filled the area between the taxiway and the terminal and then out to the runway. It all had to be cleared, but task one was to clear enough so that planes—particularly the Beast—could land. At just under a mile long and a hundred feet wide, the runway would take at least ten trips to fully clear. Depending on the quantity of refuse, maybe more. If Ray was on his way, I only had a few hours.

The Cat pushed aside the organic matter that held the water and drove through the debris with ease. The first pass up the runway took fifteen minutes as I just drove straight down the middle and let the sand and muck push to the sides. It was over a foot deep in some areas. The trip back down was more difficult, as I had to load and dump the scoop repeatedly to avoid re-covering the path I'd already cleared. That leg took forty-five minutes. Between the two trips, there was approximately twenty feet of cleared area down the middle of the runway. The Beast's wheels could fit within that width but just barely and with no margin for error.

Ray would be an hour out by now, so I turned the Cat back up the runway, zigged, zagged, dumped the muck, and continued to work my way toward the end. I was soaked with sweat, foul and smelly from the last twenty-four hours of hell, and my mouth was so parched it hurt. When I was two-thirds finished with the third scrape, a familiar sound filled the quiet sky.

Rotary engines.

The Beast approached from the east—dammit!

I put the Cat in neutral, climbed up on top of the roll bar, and waved wildly.

"Go around, Ray! Go around! Don't land from this direction!"

His angle of attack was aimed at the uncleared end of the runway. He must have seen me or recognized the mess below. He added power and peeled off to the south.

I jumped back down into the seat and sped forward to finish the scrape. The Beast wouldn't normally need the full length of the runway, but the military might send in assistance and its planes were bigger. I glanced over my shoulder and saw the Beast now approaching from the west. I steered the Cat down the taxiway and carved single path like I'd done on the first trip up the runway. Trucks could use that to unload supplies.

My lips bent into a smile as the Beast glided over the end of the runway and set down solidly on the cleared path. Loose sand flew up and trailed after in a wake of dust until she slowed halfway down the tarmac. Ray hesitated, no doubt unsure where to park, so I waved him toward the eastern end.

Back in the Rover, I drove down to retrieve Ray and Scarlet. My heart was racing, probably because I hadn't seen Scarlet in so long.

I pulled the Rover up to the Beast's port side. The hatch popped open and Scarlet jumped out. She had on khaki shorts and a khaki safari shirt just like she used to wear when we were on archaeological digs. I killed the Rover and stepped out. Scarlet's and my eyes caught, and next thing I knew we'd run toward each other and crashed into a hug.

"Hey, stranger," she said.

I felt too much to say anything at first. I hadn't seen her since I was in jail on Tortola in the British Virgin Islands facing life in prison for a murder I hadn't committed. It was Scarlet who found the video that saved my ass.

"You look great, Red." And she did.

"Wish I could say the same. You look like something God only knows what animal dragged in. And you stink, Buck Reilly."

We laughed.

Ray stepped out of the plane adorned in his favorite red Hawaiian shirt. "We flew all the way down the Keys," he said. "Holy crap, you can't believe the destruction. Boats all over the highway, swaths of homes reduced to rubble, power lines down everywhere. It's ghastly."

I finally let go of Scarlet. Our history was complex, and it was beyond surreal to have her here.

"When did you start working with the Red Cross?" I said.

She smiled and her green eyes twinkled in the sun. "Yesterday. I knew Ray had the Grumman Goose in Spruce Creek, and as soon as the hurricane turned toward the Keys I volunteered to come down and help."

"Why the hell did you take Betty up in the storm?" Ray said.

My smile faded. I knew Ray wouldn't let go, and he deserved the truth.

"I was forced to, Ray."

"Forced?"

"At gunpoint."

"What?" They said simultaneously.

"Long story, but it involved my father and a revelation that … he actually lived here in the eighties and nineties and left some money stashed on Woman Key."

"You *flew* to Woman Key during Irma?" Ray's face pinched up tighter. "And made a water landing?"

"Pretty impressive piloting if I do say so myself."

"And you were able to take off after?"

A vision of Greg dead in the bunker popped into my head. My mouth snapped closed.

"That must have been after I spoke to you on the phone," Scarlet said. "Who had you at gunpoint?"

There was no way not to share some information, but I had to be careful in case Frank came looking for me.

"An old acquaintance of my father's who said he was owed money from back in those days."

"How come you never mentioned that your father used to live here?" Ray said.

"I just found out when I was in Virginia last week going through all his old papers. I found a map in one of his notebooks, too."

"A treasure map?" Scarlet said. "Like a junkie finding smack."

"And you found what was *on* the map?" Ray said.

Scarlet studied my raised eyebrow for a half second. "Of course he did. He's King Buck."

Hadn't heard my nickname mentioned in a positive albeit sarcastic light in a long time.

"Yeah, we found it. Couple million dollars. Frank—my father's acquaintance—took it all."

"Frank who?" Ray said.

"Let's just leave it there, okay, Ray? Frank's dangerous as they come. He tried to kill us during the storm."

"*Us?*" Scarlet said.

I sighed. "Turns out my father had a business partner down here, too, and he had a daughter. The money was—is—part hers as much as mine. Of course, he wants to keep it all."

"A daughter," Scarlet said.

"All this happened during the storm?" Ray said. "Shoot, I was just worried about you surviving the damn hurricane. Did you at least get the money back?"

"We were lucky to escape, Ray."

Every time I used the word *we*, Scarlet's oh-so-friendly expression became less friendly.

"Jade—the daughter—double-crossed me, too. Tied me up and left me to drown. Total shit show. Betty's engine blew and we nearly crashed, so I'm damn fortunate to be here with you guys now."

I liked the way that softened Scarlet's eyes.

But Jade wanted the money Frank had stolen. Hell, she wanted to kill him. Why hadn't she shown up at the La Concha like we'd planned?

After I guzzled one of their water bottles, Ray, Scarlet, and I loaded the cases of water into the back of the Rover, sat three across the front bench seat, and drove back toward the terminal. When Betty came into view, Ray stiffened.

"Drive over toward Betty," he said.

"Ray, we should—"

"My car's here. I want to check Betty out. You two can go to town."

"I'm supposed to deliver those fifty cases of water to the Little White House in Truman Annex," Scarlet said.

Ray gasped when he saw the hole in the side of the smoke-blackened port engine cowling. He jumped out before I'd come to a full stop and ran to Betty like a father who'd seen his daughter fall off her bike.

Scarlet's and my trip into town was largely silent as we observed the massive destruction Irma had unleashed on Key West. I drove up Bertha to First Avenue, crossed Roosevelt and onto Palm Avenue, past Garrison Bite—the roof of the Fly Navy building, the tallest on Key West, was hanging in shreds. We saw houseboats destroyed and barely afloat, sailboats lining the shore—it was as if nearly every boat that had been left moored off the Navy base was now aground and destroyed.

"Unbelievable," Scarlet said.

"The hotel where I live is okay, but there's no air conditioning and the windows don't open. But you're welcome to stay—"

"The Red Cross provided me with a room in Truman Annex. In a condo with windows that, as far as I know, go up." She continued to stare out at the destruction. "We'll need a lot more aid than expected."

"Phones are out."

"They gave me a sat-phone"

"Thought you just signed up yesterday?"

"The director's a friend—well—friend of Craig's. I told him I was coming and he nominated me as their advance person to work with the local team."

There it was. Craig, her ex-husband's name. I swallowed.

"Speaking of Craig—"

"Let's not go there now, Buck." She turned to face me. "I promise to tell you all about it. In fact, I need to tell you about it but not yet. Okay?"

I turned left onto Southard, glanced hard at the Green Parrot on the corner of Whitehead—the doors were open—continued on, and turned right past the security gate into Truman Annex.

"Sure."

We arrived at the Little White House, President's Truman's winter retreat, and unloaded the cases of water with help from a couple of volunteers who materialized from inside. Scarlet's room was in an upper-floor condo across the street.

"Once I've assessed the situation and discussed it with headquarters, let's plan to meet, okay?" she said.

"Fine by me," I said from inside the Rover.

"About that man, Frank—please be careful, Buck."

"Will do," I said. "Until I find him."

I drove away without looking at her expression.

34

TIME TO FIND JADE. I PARKED THE ROVER AT THE LA CONCHA and checked with Lindy. She'd never appeared. What the hell?

"The list of dead is up to *fifty*," he said.

"We're all fools."

With that I walked out the front door. Duval Street was worse than the road I'd just been on—it looked like a movie set from *Jurassic Park*. Not grown over with vegetation but covered with it. It would have been impossible to bike through any roads, so I walked down a block and took a right on Southard. Another block over to the Green Parrot, whose doors were open.

A half dozen people sat around the bar.

"Come on in, survivor. Free beer," the bartender said. "We made it."

My eyes scanned the room. The old bar was intact, but there was nobody else in the back half. Just this hearty half dozen. I sat on a stool. It was a different bartender than the guy from Cudjoe Key. He slid a plastic cup of tap beer in front of me.

It was warm but tasted good.

"I was with Jade Diaz during the storm," I said.

"Thought Jade evacuated."

"You haven't seen her today?"

He shook his head. "Hasn't come in here. Could use her help if we're going to stay open. Ownership wants us to refresh the aid workers."

"We were supposed to meet up earlier, but she didn't show."

"Jade's an independent one." He extended his hand. "Shawn Ryan."

"Buck Reilly." I took the firm grip. "Maybe her place got damaged. You know where she lives?"

"Only that it's an old Conch house. Most have been around a long time, seen plenty of storms. House is in Old Town, so can't be far from here."

"We were at another friend's house—another old Conch house," I said. "You know Eleanor Graves?"

"Related to Frank Graves?"

"Ex-wife."

"Jade's mentioned him, but old-time locals don't come in here much. Ex-con, as I recall, dope smuggler. Back from the days of Bum Farto, square grouper, and cocaine cowboys. Legendary shit. Wish I'd been born then."

"Long fall for Frank. Works at the Butterfly Conservancy now."

The bartender laughed. "Most of those old smugglers did time, lost everything, and died broke. The business is back, just a new high-tech generation."

Drug smuggling had indeed ratcheted up in the Keys. Several large busts had happened offshore, and product—typically bales of cocaine—had washed up on the islands. More square grouper but a more potent variety.

"Maybe the old-timers are back in business," I said.

"Mostly Russians and crazed Mexicans now."

Characters had offered me large sums of money to charter Betty or the Beast for illicit cargo, and while I'd bent or broken my share of rules, the month I'd spent in prison in the BVI had cured me of any notion of a fast payday with a load of dope. It did give me an idea, though. I wondered how Currito made it through the storm.

"Maybe Jade just went to find some food," I said.

"I doubt Five Brothers is open. That's her go-to spot. Loves the Cuban mixes there. I prefer the sandwiches at Sandy's, but you can't beat her three-minute walk to Five Brothers."

I smiled. "True."

After a couple of long swigs I killed the beer, slapped a five down, and headed back outside. Five Brothers was also on Southard, five or six blocks away. Amazing how we could adjust to our environment no matter the condition. I'd nearly become numb to the stripped and fallen trees here in postapocalyptic Key West.

How had my other Conch friends made it through the storm? All communications were down, but I was sure Lenny, Pastor Peebles, Truck and Bruiser Lewis, Currito, and a few others had stayed behind.

I crossed Elizabeth Street.

The new journals we'd found contained more phone numbers. Some were from overseas, with 011 prefixes followed by the two-digit country code 57, then a city code and subsequent seven-digit numbers. They were probably numbers in one of the countries my father had noted in his previous journals. South American drug distribution points from back in the day. Would anybody answer if I called them now? Would anybody remember Crazy Charlie? Or Tommy Diaz? Would a number lead to former leaders of Los Pepes? They'd been forced to disband shortly after Pablo Escobar was murdered, since their job was largely done. Not that it put an end to the narco-traffickers or tyranny in the banana republics, but the most violent terrorist organization that had ever existed before Al Qaeda had been snuffed out.

Everything I'd known and believed to be my foundation had been turned upside down. I now lived in an upside-down world. Opposites were real, lies were truth, and the unbelievable was …

Shit.

I crossed William Street. Five Brothers Grocery, a family-owned bodega that had been in Key West for decades, was another few blocks ahead on the cemetery side of Grinnell. Shawn said she lived within a three-minute walk of Five Brothers. It was closed, so I walked two blocks past, turned right on White and then on Angela and again on

Frances. The houses were so close together I'd already counted twenty-seven. Eight blocks would be more than a hundred homes.

This was foolish. I'd have to see Jade to know which house was hers. Would any of my local friends who'd stayed on-island know her? Several might. It was a small community when it came to Conchs.

And one person stood out as the best place to start.

35

I WALKED TOWARD THE FENCED PERIMETER OF THE CEMETERY. A few above-ground crypts had been toppled, but they were intact, thank God, their contents inside them. Rather than walk past Eleanor's house, I took Elizabeth to Petronia.

A harsh grating noise became louder as I walked up the street toward Blue Heaven. The gates were open, and when I walked through them I saw where the shrill sound came from.

Chain saws.

Several people were huddled over what looked like a downed tree in the middle of the restaurant—actually a massive branch, I saw as I got closer. One was Lenny Robinson, Blue Heaven bartender, city councilman, and potential mayoral candidate. An outspoken and irreverent voice for Conchs and newbies alike, all of whom suffered many of the same costs and challenges of living in a tourist-dominated hot spot.

Lenny's shirt and black skin were covered with yellow sawdust.

"You should be wearing eye protection." I shouted above the saw.

Lenny looked up. His thousand-watt smile followed. He turned off the chain saw.

"Heard you stayed behind, crazy bastard," he said.

"You do okay? Willy? Church of the Redeemer?"

"Steeple got blown off and there's water damage and shit, but Willy has an army cleaning it up right now. La Concha still standing?"

We exchanged news from around the island and the Keys. Most of it worse than what I'd heard already.

"Planes survive? Last Resort Charter and Salvage still in business?"

"Ray just flew the Beast back down."

"And your other bucket of bolts that nearly killed us that time? Betty?"

"Not so good." I hesitated. I needed Lenny's help but didn't want to put him in danger. "But her trouble wasn't storm-related."

"Shit, man. Lucky she didn't get blown apart. I seen pictures from St. Martin with planes flipped over like toys."

"Betty blew an engine during the height of the storm."

His eyebrows curled up. "You flew in the storm? Wait a minute, man. I mean, I know you're one crazy white boy, but what the hell?"

"I was kidnapped at gunpoint and forced to take a local lunatic out to an island for him to dig up some shit he was worried about losing."

"What the hell? Local? Who was it, man? We'll take care of the SOB *tout-de-suite*."

"We'll get to that, trust me. I appreciate your help, but first things first. There was a local woman with me. I need to make sure she's safe."

"What's her name?"

"Jade Diaz, she's a barten—"

"Sweet Jade? You kidding me? She's a wild one. Fine, too."

"So you know her."

"We grew up together, man. Always wanted to tap that. You and her an item?"

Before I could answer, he unlocked the door on the bar and reemerged with a bottle of Pilar rum and two glasses.

"You look and smell like you need a drink. And I have a feeling I need one before you tell me any more. Kidnapped? Shit. Jade? Damn, boy."

Lenny was shocked at the edited and redacted version of my father's back story and connection to Jade's father. And Frank Graves.

"Frank Graves? He's just punk-ass white trash. He and his batty old wife—"

"Ex-wife."

"Whatever. They still together in many ways, and both are frozen in the old days—mentally. They been a ball and chain around Jade's neck her whole life. Wasn't obvious until we was in our twenties, since we was all party-crazy before, know what I mean? But Jade was a little extra crazy, man, thanks to them Graveses."

"We can talk more about Frank later," I said. "I need to know where he lives before he can escape up the Keys, but for now where does Jade live? I need to check on her."

"Can't believe Frank tried to drown her, man. They was like family, crazy or not."

"Where does she live?"

Lenny scratched his poor excuse of a goatee. "Heard she bought a house a while back, but not like we still hang out, man." Lenny leaned closer. "She and I kind of had a thing going on in high school. Never nailed her, though."

"Who would know where she lives?"

"Come around in a couple hours and I'll have answers. About that asshole Frank, too."

I left Blue Heaven and headed south. Frank was in deeper shit than he knew.

36

THE CHURCH OF THE REDEEMER'S STEEPLE lay in the middle of Thomas Street. Chunks of wood siding had peeled partially off the building, and the front corner of the roof had been crushed under the steeple's weight.

Reverend Willy Peebles stood with his hands on his hips, barking orders to a dozen people scurrying around to pick up pieces. Others hammered at new boards or peeled-off hurricane shutters. It appeared there were two men atop a ladder stapling a blue sheet of plastic over the damaged roof. Actually, it was just Truck Lewis, I realized as I got closer. He was the size of two men.

"Cut the damaged boards off a foot before where they're broken." Willy's voice was loud above the din. "Don't cut the studs!"

"Church took a hit," I said when I walked up to him.

"The building took a hit. The Church is indomitable." He scowled. "You here to help?"

"I can lend a hand—"

"Help Bruiser take those sandbags to the shed out back. The way this storm season's going, there's more to come."

Bruiser Lewis, Truck's older brother and a former boxer who'd once had a title shot only to lose in a decision, walked by with a fifty-pound sandbag under each arm. I hesitated. Would Willy know anything about Jade or Frank Graves? Bruiser spotted me.

"You still here, Reilly? Thought you'd of left on one of them old planes."

I struggled to carry a single bag of sand—my shoulder screamed—and followed Bruiser around to the back of the church. He handled his bags as if they were pillows.

"Got too busy here to get out, then it was too late," I said.

Bruiser dropped the two sandbags onto a pile of at least twenty others. "Can't thank you enough for getting some of the old-timers out before the storm."

We walked back out front and collected more sandbags.

"You know Jade Diaz?" I said. "Used to be a dancer at Bare Assets?"

He glanced back over his shoulder and leaned closer.

"Keep it down, man." He glanced around again. "Yeah, I know Jade. Fine-looking woman. Tough as nails. Haven't seen in her in a long time, though. Why you ask?"

"Long story short, turns out our fathers used to be running mates back in the eighties. Yesterday, a crazy bastard who used to hang with them tried to kill us."

"Kill? Say what?"

"Name's Frank Graves. Former dope smuggler, did twenty years. Has a chip on his shoulder about our fathers, wanted to take it out on us. Left us to drown tied up in a flooding hole, but we escaped. He had a gun and I didn't, so we just hightailed it out."

"Let's go get the son of a bitch." Bruiser's voice was loud.

I noticed Willy watching us.

"Not yet, but I may need your help at some point."

Willy walked toward us.

"You know where Jade lives?" I said. "I'm just worried Frank will go hurt her."

"Shoot, Buck. Never went to her house. Heard she bought one in Old Town. Can't remember the street."

"Work to do here, men," Willy said. "You can chitchat later."

"Sorry, Willy, but I need to run," I said. "Thanks, Bruiser."

"Grinnell!" he shouted. "I heard from someone who lives on Hibiscus Lane that she bought an old Conch house on Grinnell, around the corner."

I gave Bruiser a thumbs-up. "I'll keep you posted."

It took fifteen minutes to get to the corner of Southard and Grinnell and another fifteen to walk both sides of Grinnell between the corner and Fleming. Hibiscus Lane was right in the middle of the block. There were twenty houses in total, all of which seemed to be evacuated. None had any sign of Jade. The wind continued to whip the trees around, rain occasionally came down in sheets, and daylight was quickly fading.

Soggy and spent, I made my way back to the La Concha. Lindy had candles set up around the lobby, and light flickered against the white walls. On the counter were a flashlight, four candles, and a note: "Buck, Take these and be safe on the stairs. See you tomorrow. PS, you have a visitor."

Visitor? What the hell? Frank? Jade?

I searched around the lobby for Lindy but couldn't find him.

Crap.

The stairwell and the corridors were dark and spooky. It again felt like an end-of-the-world kind of movie. I extinguished my flashlight. If it was Frank, surprise would be my only weapon.

I hesitated by the door, which was cracked open. I touched the handle, and the hinge let out a slight creak.

"Buck, is that you?" A woman's voice.

I pushed the door open. "Jade—I've been searching everywhere—"

"Ahh, sorry. Just me."

"Scarlet. I'm sorry, I thought you were staying at—"

"Truman Annex, I am. But I felt bad for rushing off earlier."

"No problem. I mean, great—I'm glad you're here."

The heat in the room was stifling. The temperature on the sixth floor was in the eighties. Sleep would be miserable tonight. I could smell myself and wished above all else I could take a shower, but the water mains from Miami were still shut down. Who knew how long it would take to get the water back on? I had an idea.

"We pretty much have the hotel to ourselves. I feel and smell disgusting. Let's go down to the swimming pool."

"Great idea."

At the pool, we both stripped to our underwear and got in. The water was ambient temperature but felt amazing. Scarlet appreciated my having brought soap and shampoo.

"We'll be squeaky-clean all over."

Scarlet was the one person I'd always been able to trust. Even after I let her down and possibly broke her heart, she had still come to my rescue. I told her the whole story of my Dad's notebooks as we soaked in the pool, what I'd learned here in the Keys, the bunker out on Woman Key and who was in it. She took it all in stride.

I told her the details of Frank's attempt to kill me and Jade, how we escaped, and our finding the other half of the tunnel.

"With additional notebooks," I said.

"Any more maps in them?"

"A few, but they're more like city maps, not treasure maps. Mostly just more names, figures, and some phone numbers—overseas ones."

A flashback to our e-Antiquity days made me smile. Scarlet was the brains behind many of our discoveries. She was extraordinary at research and a great co-strategist in the field.

"You want to take a look at them? They're upstairs."

"I'd like to see them—as long as Jade won't be upset."

"There's no reason on Earth Jade would be upset and you know it."

With that we ran, soaking wet—we'd forgotten towels—back into the hotel and up the steps.

37

THE NAMES IN THE NOTEBOOKS WERE THE SAME ONES I'd found in Virginia. But these had figures with them, and many had several dates noted. Like a diary of times they'd met.

"You say these were people in Colombia?" Scarlet said.

"And Cuba, Peru, and Panama."

On the back page she read the international phone numbers. Three of the numbers started with 011, followed by 57 and then 4, and one number had the number 1 after 57.

"Zero-one-one is the code to exit the U.S. phone system," she said.

"Right, but with my computer down I'm not sure about the country and city codes. Do you have your sat-phone with you?"

She reached into her purse on the counter and removed a small black phone with a long antenna.

"It can pull up low-bandwidth Internet." She glanced up after a quick search. "We should've known. Colombia is country code 57, and Medellín is city code 4."

"Then city code 1 must be in Bogotá."

"That's right," she said. "You think the numbers may lead to some of the people on the lists?"

"Pablo Escobar's old number, for all we know." I hesitated. "Mind if I use your phone to see if they still work?"

"The Red Cross owes you that much since Ray flew me down here."

I started with the exchanges in Medellín. The first number led to a recording, and even though neither of us spoke Spanish—I'd started studying it online—we were pretty sure it stated that the number was no longer in service.

The second number was answered by a man who spoke in a whisper.

"*Dime.*"

That word I knew. It meant: tell me. "Hello, can you tell me whose number this is?" I said.

Scarlet shook her head. The man on the other end hung up.

"What was I supposed to say?"

The third number just rang and rang.

The last number was the one in Bogotá. Someone picked up after one ring.

There was a long pause. "United States Embassy," a man finally said. "Can I help you?"

Scarlet and I exchanged a glance. She waved her hand in a circle.

"Yes, hello, is this the embassy in Bogotá, Colombia?"

Scarlet rolled her eyes.

"Who's calling please?"

"I'm, ah, looking into a missing persons case."

The man on the other end of the line hesitated. "This is a private line within the Embassy. The main number is—"

"I was given this number by a friend." I paused. "He hasn't used it since 1993."

Silence. Was that breathing on the line?

"Hello?" I said.

"Who am I speaking with?"

Scarlet nodded at me. What the hell?

"My name's Buck—Charles B. Reilly III, to be precise."

All I could hear was the sound of fingers pounding a keyboard until he came back onto the line.

"You said 1993?"

"That's right."

"Are you related to former Undersecretary of the Department of State Charles B. Reilly Jr.?"

"He's my father."

"Interesting," the man said. "Well, son, you've reached a secure number here at the Embassy. Still looking for a missing person?"

What?

"Kind of, yes. Secure line?"

"What are you after?" the man said.

I hit the "end" button on the sat-phone.

"Wow," I said.

"You think the government's been monitoring that number all these years?"

I hesitated for a long moment while the wheels spun in my head.

"I don't know," I said finally, "but I'm going to find out."

"How are you going to do that?"

I wiped fresh sweat off my brow.

"I'm going to fly to Colombia."

Scarlett's eyes nearly popped out of her head. "What the hell for?"

"All my life I've looked up to my father. He was my role model. And then I find out he was a drug smuggler and possibly a murderer associated with Los Pepes." I shook my head. "The airport here will soon be full of military and other relief planes, and I won't be able to do any more than heft boxes, serve food, and hand out water bottles."

"Something wrong with that?" Scarlet said.

"And the road up the Keys will be closed for days, at least, so it gives me a window before Frank can escape."

"A window for what?"

"To fill in the blanks on my father's drug-smuggling history." Scarlet gave me a long look and nodded. I jumped up and pulled my backpack and flight bag out of the closet.

"Speaking of truth," she said, "I wasn't totally honest with you on why I came here."

"Not the Red Cross?" I stuffed a fresh pair of underwear and T-shirt into my backpack.

A smile flashed across her face. "That, yes, but I also wanted—needed to talk to you."

"I'll be back in a couple days, Scarlet, I promise."

"It can wait."

"I'm sorry, Scarlet. What I've found out about my father has me crazy. We can talk now if you want."

She held a hand up. "No, it's waited quite a while. A few more days won't matter."

Damn. Scarlet came here to talk to me and I was packing my bag for a witch hunt.

She picked up her purse and turned toward the door. I grabbed her shoulder and slowly turned her around.

"I'm very glad you're here. Do you want to stay?"

"No, no, no."

"I'm sorry."

"I understand. It's okay."

She stared unflinchingly into my eyes and I flashed back to the times when we were in remote jungles and deserts on archaeological digs by day and sharing my bed by night.

"Just be careful for once—will you, Buck?"

"You betcha, Red."

With that she pulled free and disappeared into the dark corridor.

Smooth move, Reilly.

SECTION 5

CRIME AND PUNISHMENT

38

WITH RAY FLOYD'S RELUCTANT ASSISTANCE, I was able to refuel the Beast and skedaddle out of Key West before sunrise the next morning as the first C-130 loaded with relief supplies appeared on the horizon. To beat the military taking over the airport, I had Ray file my flight plan for me by radio from Betty after I left. Hell, I'd used the front-end loader to clear the landing path on the runway to facilitate entry and exit, so that should have earned me the right to go even though the airport was closed.

Ray was correct in thinking my flight plan was insane. It would take fourteen hours and three fuel stops to cover the over sixteen hundred nautical miles to Bogotá by sunset. And that was if everything went okay.

The Beast flew strong, and the initial leg to Cozumel, an island I knew well, took just under three hours. With the sunrise at my back, the oval green and brown island was set like a jewel amid the turquoise waters. Gray Mayan ruins peered out from wooded canopies, and it was hard not to let the sights distract me from the landing checklist.

The first time I'd landed at Cozumel International Airport was in a Gulfstream G-IV rental from Net Jet back in the dusk of e-Antiquity. Here I was now aboard a seventy-five-year-old flying boat. I paid cash for the fuel and, once given clearance, took off south toward Golosón International Airport in La Ceiba, Honduras, two hundred ninety nautical miles away.

I set the Beast down on Runway 7, nearly ten thousand feet long. I was lucky to gain a reasonably fast fuel stop and a quick exit south toward Tocumen International Airport in Panama City, Panama another two hundred ninety miles south. Two hours later we set down there and I stretched my legs while the Beast was refueled. Fatigue had set in but daylight was burning fast and I didn't want to try navigating around the mountains of Bogotá at night, so after a strong coffee and a splash of water in my face, we were once again flying south.

After another two and a half hours, the Beast and I were on fumes when given clearance to land at Bogotá's Eldorado International Airport. I set the Beast down hard, just as the sun kissed the peak of mountains and the light quickly faded away. I cut power to the port engine, and limped up to Slot 13 at Central Charter de Colombia just as my fuel ran dry and the starboard engine fluttered to a stop.

Good grief.

I'd asked the taxi driver to swing by the U.S. Embassy, which consumed an entire city block. Fenced and heavily guarded with Old Glory flapping in a steady breeze, it looked as impenetrable as a maximum-security prison. It had to be, given the violence of the narco era in Colombia and the lingering resentment of U.S. meddling in the country's internal affairs.

My plan was to go there tomorrow morning and use my father's history as an undersecretary of state to find out where the number I'd called yesterday had been answered.

"Driver, take me to the Hilton Bogotá."

I'd see what I could learn tomorrow in Bogotá and then head to Medellín to track down the other phone number that was still active.

"*Dime*," the man who'd answered the phone there had said.

Exactly. Tell me. I need to know the truth. If I better understand what my father did back then, I may be able to better come to terms with it.

The Hilton Bogotá was a dark monolith on a busy street. My boat shoes squeaked on the black terrazzo floor in the stone-walled lobby.

Once checked in, I headed to Room 714, where the phone was ringing as I opened the door.

Had I left my credit card or passport at reception?

"Yes?" I said.

"Long way from home, hotshot."

No. It can't be.

"Special Agent T. Edward Booth here, in case you forgot my voice—"

"How'd you know where I am? And what the hell do you want?"

He had hounded me for years after my parents' death, claiming to have evidence related to e-Antiquity's collapse that could put me in jail. Booth had used that knowledge to force me to help with investigations beyond the FBI's jurisdiction, the successes of which propelled him up the federal ladder off my shoulders.

"I'm calling to do you a favor, so relax."

"Why would you do me a favor? And how'd you know I was here? Are you still tracking me?"

"The minute you called last night—"

"The guy said it was the U.S. Embassy. A private line—"

"It set off alarm bells deep inside our security apparatus that led to my phone waking me up in the middle of the night."

I bit my lip.

"They placed you on a watch list, and lo and behold, less than twenty-four hours later, you show up at Customs in Bogotá."

"Why would me calling that number cause this chain reaction?"

"I'm your handler—"

"Not anymore, dammit!"

Booth paused a moment. "Your father, Reilly—"

"He's dead."

"He has history down there."

Crap. The FBI must have a file on Dad from back in the day.

"I don't know what you're talking about."

A long exhale caused distortion on the line and triggered my gag reflex at the memory of Booth's bad breath.

"Play it however you want, Reilly, but to make myself clear, I know the truth."

I couldn't breathe.

"Do *you* want to know the truth about your father?"

"Yes."

"Then do what I tell you and no more questions or bullshit. Go downstairs. There's a black Chevy Suburban parked out front. Get in the back—"

"You going to make me disappear, Booth?"

"I said no more questions. There's a man in the Suburban who can answer yours. Then it's up to you how you want to play it."

"Who's the man?"

Click.

"Booth?"

Shit.

I jumped up and peered out the window. There was indeed a black Suburban parked in front of the hotel. There were also two black Mercedes sedans, one parked in front of the Suburban and one behind it.

My heart raced like I'd guzzled a gallon of Cuban coffee.

I grabbed my backpack and ran to the door.

39

INSIDE THE LOBBY WAS A BALD, HEAVY MAN WEARING KHAKIS, a blue button-down shirt, and horn-rim glasses. I noticed him because he raised a palm—telling me to halt—as I approached the front door.

"Charles B. Reilly III?"

"That's me. Who are you?"

"Agent Blutarsky. We spoke on the phone last night. You called me." He seemed but faintly interested, like he confronted American visitors in Colombian hotels on a daily basis.

"I assume you're the answer man that Booth—FBI Special Agent T. Edward Booth—told me about?"

"What are you after in Bogotá?"

"Information."

"About what?" His expression remained bored.

"My father."

He glanced behind me and viewed my backpack.

"What's in there?"

"Underwear, socks, T-shirts, names of dead narcos in some of my father's private notebooks."

His eyes narrowed and then he nodded as if to himself—I didn't think it was a sniper somewhere in the distance.

"Let's get in the Suburban." He began walking.

I instinctively balled my fists. "Why should I trust you?"

He peered back over his shoulder. "Because you have nobody else."

Good point.

I followed him—with a glance at the Mercedes in front of the Suburban, but the windows were darkly tinted. I climbed into the backseat. There was a driver and a man in the passenger seat. Neither turned to face us.

"Let me see the notebooks," Blutarsky said.

The rear zipper pocket of my backpack contained two of the notebooks. I pulled them out slowly.

"I want these back. There's more, and depending on how things go, I could let you see them, too."

"They in your hotel room at the La Concha?"

I handed him one from the tunnel in Key West, but it wasn't the one with the phone numbers. I'd left that one at the La Concha.

Shit—damn.

Blutarsky paged through the notebook without saying a word. His expression never changed. The men in the front seats stared forward, occasionally checking their side mirrors.

"Where'd you find this?"

"Hidden in Key West, apparently near where my father once lived. I never knew he lived there until a week ago."

He slapped the notebook closed and handed it back. His open hand lingered. I passed him one from Middleburg but without the map. It did list names of dead men and countries throughout South America.

"What else have you learned about your father's activities from those days?"

I'd practiced a response to this inevitable question during the flight down.

"Only that he had a friend who disappeared and was reportedly killed in Colombia in 1992 and that he came looking for him."

Blutarsky gave me a long stare.

"His friend have a name?"

"Tommy Diaz."

He shrugged.

"What do you have for me, Agent Blutarsky?"

"I have to speak with someone in the car behind us," he said. "I'll be right back."

Five long minutes later the back door opened next to me. Blutarsky stood there alone.

"Follow me."

We walked to the Mercedes 500 sedan behind the Suburban. Its windows were darkly tinted, too, but I could see two men in dark glasses in the front seat. The back door swung open and Blutarsky waved a hand toward the interior.

"Dean Wormer can shed some light on your questions."

He waited until I sat in the backseat before closing the door.

A handsome silver-haired man in a silver sharkskin suit smiled at me as if he were meeting his new son-in-law for the first time.

"Charles B. Reilly III. Buck, it's a pleasure to meet you." Looking at his face, I believed him. For whatever reason, it *was* a pleasure.

He held his hand out. His grip was firm, his hand smooth.

"Dean Wormer, huh? Guess that makes me Otter or Flounder?"

"You have correctly discerned that that's not my real name." He smiled. "Agent Booth spoke highly of you."

A laugh burst from my lips. "Are we going to continue this charade or are you going to tell me what's going on?"

"Actually, Booth said you're pretty crazy."

"What's that supposed to mean?"

"Charles B. Reilly III, are you a Crazy Charlie like your father?"

He knew my father's nickname. "Depends on the situation. Now, who are you, really?"

He sat back and drew in a deep breath.

"My birth name was Thomas James Diaz. Your father was my friend—"

My mouth fell open.

"As in Tommy Diaz?"

"That's right."

I reached for my breast pocket, and the driver spun around.

"What are you doing?" he said.

"Just getting a picture out of my shirt pocket, fellas. Relax."

With two fingers I pulled a pair of photos from my pocket. I handed them to Diaz. A huge smile crossed his face and wrinkles appeared in the corners of his eyes.

"Damn, we were good-looking." He smiled at the pic of himself, my dad, and Frank Graves. Then his smile grew even wider. "I took this other one of your father. We were out on Woman Key, a few miles off Key West."

Woman Key. Damn. So much of my family history had been lies. I believed Tommy Diaz, but his younger self in the photo didn't look *that* much like he did now. I wanted some concrete reassurance. "Can you show me some identification, please?"

The smile faded as he pulled a badge out of his breast pocket, flashed it at me, and slapped it closed. All I saw was "US Special Agent."

"I have a lot to tell you, Buck."

"And I have a few things to tell you, Tommy."

40

"I WAS A DEEP-COVER DEA AGENT IN THE EIGHTIES AND NINETIES."

Say *what*?

"I was stationed in Miami and Key West but spent a lot of time in Colombia and Latin America." He paused. "In fact, my associate Blutarsky says you have a notebook that includes many of my former contacts' names."

"Dead ones."

"Alas, it was a difficult era."

Understatement of the millennium.

"And my father?"

"Crazy Charlie." He smiled. "He was my partner—interagency contact, to be precise."

My heart rate clicked up a notch. "What agency?"

"Central Intelligence. He was the best—in fact, we were quite a team."

A surge of emotion pressed me back into my seat.

Dad wasn't a smuggler! CIA!

"I was so very sorry to hear of his death, Buck."

My father was dead and Tommy Diaz was back from the grave. The world was right side up again. Tommy waited quietly through the couple of minutes it took to find my voice.

"Word had it that you were dead, too, Tommy."

"Like I said, it was deep cover."

"My father supposedly went to Colombia to avenge your death, and based on what I've pieced together in his notebooks, he was affiliated with Los Pepes."

Diaz smiled again, his white teeth bright against a closely trimmed silver beard. "Outstanding! Our deception remains intact even today. I can't tell you how important that has been in the war on drugs—how impactful your father's and my efforts were. Continue to be even today."

"Impactful. Good word."

He smiled. "I'll tell you what only a few people know. As your father's son, I trust you completely, as I did him. Escobar was a paranoid lunatic, and out of the blue he believed I couldn't be trusted. He issued a death warrant on me. The story was that I was killed by one of his men high up in the organization. The assassin's name isn't important, but he was a mole—my mole. We fabricated my death. The story was that he exposed and killed me, which brought him closer to Pablo Escobar. Immediately thereafter your father was able to use Agency intel to create a coordinated effort with the leaders of Los Pepes—"

"The Castaño brothers and their band of brutal murderers."

"Tortured times, Buck. The reign of terror was unlike anything that had been seen before. By then the Colombian government was happy to look the other way. The police were, too, except for those on Escobar's payroll. The national police had lost over a thousand men and women. They supported the joint cooperation."

"*Joint* meaning CIA, DEA, Colombian police—"

"Search bloc is what the elite Colombian police were referred to then."

"Combined with paramilitary hit men."

Diaz sighed. "Let's just say the results spoke for themselves. Colombia had been under siege for a decade. Car bombings, kidnappings, a commercial jetliner blown out of the sky, and billions of dollars of grass and coke smuggled into the United States."

"Those persecuted by Pablo Escobar took over?" I said.

"The perfect battle plan. It was war, and because we'd been playing by the rules we'd lost every fight. We had no choice, the Colombian people had no choice—their politicians had approved extradition of the narcos into the war far too late."

"So you and my father were in the middle of it all?"

Diaz leaned closer. "Your father and I were two of three men who could tell you what Escobar's expression was the moment he died."

Good Lord.

"Los Pepes was closed down shortly after that. Some of the leaders and operatives refused to quit, so we had to reel them in—"

"But you were undercover!"

"Most people who knew me before my supposed death were either in jail or dead by then. I go by Emilio Navarro now—have since 1992. So, yes, for all intents and purposes, Tommy Diaz was dead."

"This is beyond bizarre."

"It's life on the front lines of the war on drugs. Your father was a hero, Buck. He was offered any post the Agency had, and he chose to go to State—"

"He was still CIA while undersecretary of state?"

Diaz sat back. "I can't jeopardize any current operations—"

"You said you trusted me. My father's been dead nearly ten years. My mother, too."

"I know. Tragic, indeed."

A light popped on in my brain. "Could their deaths be related to his activities here in Colombia? CIA activities?"

"Investigations into that possibility were made, believe me. Nothing was found. There was no chatter or glory hounds taking credit for their deaths."

I studied Diaz's face. He had the best poker player's eyes I'd ever seen. "When was the last time you spoke to my father?"

"Nineteen ninety-seven. June, to be exact." He paused. "Sad thing about this business, once colleagues get reassigned, you generally lose touch unless your investigations intersect. There's no Facebook for undercover agents."

He was scrutinizing my face again. Mine was more of a go-fish face than a poker face.

"So you found the tunnels in Key West?" he said.

"That's right. One led from my dad's old house and the other led from yours. Not much there—those notebooks, some cash, some old weed, and a gun."

"Nothing else?"

"I did find something else." I paused. "Your daughter, Jade."

I couldn't begin to read the expression in Tommy's eyes.

"Jade. I haven't seen her in over twenty-five years." He shifted in his seat.

"She thinks you're dead. Describing her as bitter would be an understatement."

He ran a palm through his silver hair. "My greatest sacrifice—"

"How convenient," I said. "Martyrdom."

"Excuse me?"

"She's your daughter, Tommy. Been through hell, as far as I can see. I've only known her a couple of weeks, but with all the old-timers in Key West thinking you were an assassinated smuggler and her mother a junkie who overdosed, her life's been a shit sandwich."

A long moment passed. Tommy's poker face was now marred by tears at the corners of each eye. Guilt tore at my heart. Who was I to judge a man for his mistakes?

"I had no choice. Once I'd been condemned in Colombia, the cartel would have killed my family for vengeance—"

"You said yourself that most everyone who knew you was dead—"

"Not everyone! You don't understand—these people are monsters. I couldn't come back from the dead—"

"Why didn't you send for her? Especially after her mother died—"

"Money was sent to her aunt—"

"That didn't work out. Your old partner, Frank Graves—"

"Frank was not my partner! He was a cutout. He had people who'd unload the drugs and take it all to transfer stations, where unbeknownst to them it was destroyed. It was the perfect cover. We actually imported drugs. We had credibility. But the drugs never made it to the streets."

"Until you died and then my father disappeared. After that Frank went solo."

"And got what he deserved."

"You know what else Frank and Eleanor his ex-wife got? They got your daughter. They had more to do with Jade's upbringing than anyone."

"Frank was in prison—"

"Which made it even worse. Jade's foster father was a convict. Who's been out for quite a while."

By the expression on Tommy's face, it was clear he hadn't kept tabs on his daughter. His life was the game, the pursuit, and the high-stakes war against the billionaire drug cartels. In that moment, a feeling of warmth passed through me.

Gratitude.

My father had taken the high road. Yes, he'd been in it up to his eyeballs, but he'd downshifted to a semi-normal life, undercover or not. He was there for us, his family.

"I could never explain this in a way you'd understand." Tommy had turned sideways to face me. The streetlight outside the car lit his silver hair, beard, and suit. He was glowing. "I never imagined you and Jade would meet."

"History brought us together. Yours and my father's. I found other notebooks at his house in Virginia, and one had a map."

"Half a map," he said.

"And Jade had your half. She spent her entire life trying to crack it in the hope that you left her something more than a bad name. The maps led us to the tunnels."

"And Woman Key?" he said.

"Yours, too, I suppose."

He squirmed in his seat. "Government property."

"It nearly got me killed, Tommy. An innocent man was murdered—a friend of mine, in front of my goddamned eyes!"

"By who?"

I shook my head. "Your cutout. Frank Graves. Said you and my old man never paid him. He'd helped Jade search for that money ever since he got out of prison."

"How'd he like it when she met the famous treasure hunter?"

"Frank got greedy—he has your dirty government money now—and tried to kill us. Tied us up in a place where we'd be sure to drown. But he knows we escaped, so she's in danger, Tommy. May already have been recaptured or worse."

"I'll call the authorities—"

"That's what you'll do? Your daughter's life is in jeopardy, so you'll make a phone call?"

"You don't understand. I *can't* go back! Everything I've done—everything *we've* carefully established over decades—could all be ruined. And Jade and I would likely be killed."

My stomach sank. Gone was the slick puppeteer, his cool demeanor now cracked. No doubt Tommy Diaz was considered a legend in undercover circles by the few in the know, but in reality he was just another self-possessed workaholic who'd abandoned his family.

I reached for the door handle. "Thanks for telling me about my father. It's a relief."

"It's classified, too. Don't tell a soul." My eyes bore into his like laser beams. "About me, either," he said.

"Understood."

The door popped open silently and I slid out. Before closing it I glanced back at Tommy, suddenly appearing older, more frail, less slick and silver in the dome light.

"Your daughter needs you, Tommy," I said and slammed the door.

41

I LEFT THE NEXT MORNING. RATHER THAN CONTINUING on to Medellín, I headed back to Key West, a journey that again took all day. Ray Floyd didn't respond to any of my radio calls. Key West still had no phone service and the airport was still closed, so I had no idea what lay ahead.

Was she safe? Maybe so, if the son of a bitch had found a way to escape with our fathers'—the government's money. Tommy hadn't seemed interested in getting that back.

It had been nearly impossible to believe my father had been a drug smuggler, but a CIA agent who'd cut his teeth on the bones of narcos made sense, as did the shift to diplomacy/intelligence. I was sad that I'd never be able to discuss all that with him now that I knew, but he'd been active-duty right up to the moment he was run over on the streets of Geneva.

There was little air traffic around the Keys. When I announced my approach into Key West Airport, Air Traffic Control based in Miami instructed me to divert to there because EYW was closed.

"Negative, Control. I'm a relief plane working with the Red Cross." Ray had flown in Scarlet's water from the Red Cross, so it was nearly truthful.

"Roger, Grumman. Proceed, VFR."

Visual flight rules indeed.

I noticed an old DC-3 on the tarmac. A human chain was passing boxes of relief supplies to a truck. I wished I'd arrived with something more than enlightenment.

The Beast set down with grace. Once we taxied over to the private aviation hangar, I spotted Ray Floyd walking toward me from the DC-3. I looked around but didn't see Betty. Ray popped open the hatch as the Beast's twin rotary engines spun to a slow halt.

"Where's Betty?" I said.

"In pieces in the Conch Flyer's hangar. Total rebuild needed. Was able to radio my supplier in Alaska. Parts are on the way."

How would I pay for that?

"It's a mess in town but nothing compared to twenty-five miles up the Keys. I've been helping Scarlet—she's amazing—but all the destroyed homes, boats, and devastation are unbelievable. Hundreds of people have lost everything."

Scarlet. She'd said the other night that she wanted to talk to me.

"Has Scarlet said anything about me?"

"Like that she's still in love with you?"

I whipped around to face Ray. "She said that?"

His shit-eating grin made me cross my arms.

"No, but she kind of glows if your name comes up, like when I asked when the hell you'd be back."

I slammed the hatch closed on the Beast and locked it. The truck over by the DC-3 lumbered away loaded with relief supplies. Another truck pulled in to replace it. I recognized my friends Shawn Martin and Preston Brewer there helping out. What I should be doing.

"Has anyone come here looking for me?"

"Lenny was asking—"

"Like Jade Diaz or Frank Graves?"

"The guy who kidnapped you? No. And no women have come looking either." He nodded toward the truck that had replaced the one at the DC-3. "We could use your help with these supplies. They're for Scarlet's Red Cross efforts."

"Gotta go, Ray. I want to help, but I have to find Jade. And Frank."

"Be careful, Buck. That guy's a killer."

"Tell me about it."

42

A NATIONAL GUARD HUMVEE FULL OF TROOPS was the only other vehicle on the road. I got hard stares as it drove past. Was Key West under martial law? Too soon for police, fire, and other city or county services to have been restored.

Small groups of people were mobilized in different parts of town, their efforts punctuated by the sounds of chain saws. Piles of organic matter, junk, and demolished portions of homes and buildings lined many of the streets. The sun was out and the air hot. No running water or air conditioning relieved the suffering of the residents still here or the aid workers.

Time to return to the scene and see what I could learn.

I turned right onto Angela Street. The mahogany tree that had collapsed on us and sunk into the tunnel still hung intact at a forty-five-degree angle. There were no vehicles parked in front of Eleanor's house. I parked the Rover and got out. There was a dark hole below the mahogany tree where the edge of the road had collapsed into the tunnel, but unless you knew it was there—or had been trapped beneath it—you wouldn't realize what lay below. I tapped my pocket to make sure Greg's knife was still there and climbed slowly up Eleanor's steps, listening closely for any sounds. Her front door was wide open. I walked in without knocking.

Empty water bottles were piled atop the heaps of hoarded junk that lined the hallway. A faint rustling sound emerged from deeper inside the house. I tiptoed carefully forward. At the end of the hall, where it connected to the kitchen, I peered slowly around the corner. Eleanor was seated next to a window, reading a book.

Canned goods—Vienna sausages and tuna—were stacked high just inside the kitchen. Relief food. I pushed it over—

CRASH!

Eleanor leaped out of her rocking chair like a scalded cat.

"What the hell—you! What're you doing here?"

Her eyes had shifted from curious to furious in a split second.

"Hello, Eleanor."

"You can't just walk in here like you own the place."

"The door was open."

Her hand shot up and she pointed down the hall.

"Get out, now!"

"Your concern for my safety is heartwarming," I said.

"You're trouble—all of you—nothing but trouble."

She dropped her book on the counter and picked up a .38 caliber revolver that had been hidden behind a stack of junk. She held it at her side.

I raised my hands slowly. "Easy now, I'm here to help."

"Ha! That's funny, Buck Reilly. Help yourself to those bags of cash, you mean."

Her expression reminded me of the Wicked Witch of the West.

"Have you heard anything from Jade? Is she safe?"

She took a step toward me, the gun still at her side.

"Safe? Jade? The double-crossing, ungrateful bitch?" She waved the gun around as she spit out her words.

"Eleanor, Jade double-crossed *me* when Frank made me fly him out to Woman Key."

"Screw that—she double-crossed me! Both of them did. Tied me up and left me to starve after the storm." She nodded to a wooden chair broken into pieces on the floor behind the kitchen island. "I smashed myself against the wall until the damn chair broke apart."

"Jade and Frank are together?"

Eleanor's mouth turned downward. "You really are a sap, aren't you, Reilly? Yes, they're together—I'm not sure just *how* together they are, but given the way Frank leers at her, anything's possible. Especially since they have all that damn money."

Good grief.

"They were in on it together the whole time. We all were—against you. But then the greedy bastards turned on me—I'll kill Frank if I see him." She raised the gun.

Jade and Frank. Son of a bitch.

"You think they're still on Key West—or Stock Island? Doesn't Frank live there in a trailer?"

"While they were tying me up they were plotting to drive up the Keys in Jade's truck when they got out of here, so it depends on the roads."

"A1A is still closed from Sugarloaf to Islamorada."

"They also talked about stealing a boat—"

"Nobody's allowed on the water, either—too many sunken vessels around the island for safe navigation. The Coast Guard has everything bottled up tight."

An evil smile curled the corner of her lip up. "Then they must be stuck here like fish in a barrel." She held the gun up and pretended to shoot it.

"Where does Jade live?"

"Why should I tell you? So you can steal the money? What about—"

"How about I give you half of anything I recover and keep?"

Her eyes lit up. "Now you're talking—but how do I know if I can trust you?"

I thought of what Agent Blutarsky said to me in Bogotá. "Because you have nobody else."

She processed that for a quick second, then gave me a nod.

"Okay, you have a deal. Let's get those sons of bitches. Jade lives on Grinnell Street in a big white two-story Conch house with porches on both levels."

"That describes a lot of—"

"It's between two lanes—forget the names—and it's got one-story bungalows on both sides. You can't miss it."

The image of a large white Conch house surprised me.

"Does she rent it?"

"Owns it."

"How'd she afford that?"

"You know how long she was a stripper? Made a shitload of cash and paid minimal taxes." Eleanor's smile was that of a proud mother. "Raised that girl smart, I did."

Obviously.

"What about Frank's place if they're not at Jade's?"

"Lives in a trailer off Fifth Avenue on Stock Island near where the old drive-in movie theater was but on the other side of Fifth. Faded blue with some kind of fish mailbox out front. Probably square grouper, the dumb-ass."

We stared at each other for a long moment. She was furious, a woman scorned. I was pissed, a man double-double-crossed. But Jade had saved me from certain drowning when the tree collapsed on us and I was stuck. Why?

Time to find out.

43

TO WHAT EXTENT WERE JADE AND FRANK connected? Had her smacking his hand away when he grabbed her ass been an act? The punch he'd hit her with certainly wasn't.

Frank was unstable.

Jade was devious and a pathological liar.

Together they were a codependent nightmare. Not to mention armed and dangerous. They'd escape north as soon as they could. They had to know I'd come looking for them, so they'd be ready to go. Frank knew my plane was damaged, but would they know my other plane had returned and I'd left in it? Hopefully so, because they might not know I was back.

As badly as I wanted to drive immediately to Jade's house, my Rover was too loud and recognizable. They'd both driven in it and would hear me coming before I got anywhere near them. Instead I made my way to the La Concha, where I parked it out back. Lindy had been busy—half the parking area had been raked and swept, and a large pile of sticks and branches was stacked near the sidewalk on Whitehead Street. Lindy walked over from the side of the hotel with a rake in his hand.

"Boy, am I glad to see you," he said.

"Has a woman come looking for me? Jade Diaz?"

He shook his head. "That redhead stopped by again this afternoon asking if you were back. I sure could use your help here, Buck. The property's a mess and I—"

"Sorry, Lindy. Can't quite yet. I'm on a mission right now."

His smile soured. "Okay, man, I understand."

"I promise I'll be able to help later—tomorrow, hopefully."

"Yeah, tomorrow's fine. This mess isn't getting cleaned up overnight." He smiled. "Keys strong, though."

I looked past Lindy's dirty shirt and surveyed the rubble that now covered only half the parking lot.

"Made a lot of progress, Lindy. You're the salt of the earth."

He laughed to himself and strolled away.

My bike was still locked on the rack. It might be crazy to try to ride it through the mess of the streets, but I'd noticed that Fleming was largely cleared when I drove by. I set off with nothing more than a chip on my shoulder.

That realization gave me an idea, and I continued down Whitehead past Fleming to Petronia and turned right.

In Bahama Village I encountered more people outside working to clean the neighborhood—African Americans, Bahamian Americans, Conch Americans. There was a deeper-rooted civic pride in Bahama Village that exceeded what was evident in most of the NIMBY neighborhoods.

I pulled into Blue Heaven. No more chain saws. The bar was open and a few locals sat on stools. The sound of Lenny's voice regaled them with what was needed in Key West. I was getting used to Lenny's being a town councilman.

"Buck Reilly," he said. "Thought you'd be out with Ray and that fine redhead doing your civic duty."

I waved him to the other side of the bar.

"What's up?"

"May need some help," I said.

"You kidding me? Everybody needs help in this shit—"

"Serious help, Lenny. Frank and Jade are together. They've got the money, and as soon as the roads are open they'll be out of here faster than one of your political contributors in need of a favor."

"Jade, huh? Must be a lot of money if she's running off with that old bastard."

"It is."

"And you want it back?"

"I do."

His voice dropped to a whisper. "If I bring muscle, you'll cut us in?"

"Yes. But Frank needs to be brought to justice for murder."

"Of course." His voice was loud now. "Justice. Damn straight." I rolled my eyes. "Where they at, man?"

I told Lenny of both locations and said I was going to start out at Jade's house on Grinnell.

"Five Brothers is back open. Better get yourself fired up on a double Bucci first."

"Don't worry, I'm plenty fired up."

"I'll see what I can do," Lenny said.

He held out his fist and I bumped it—hard. He recoiled and gave me a sharp look but held his tongue.

Back on my bike I rode the wrong way up Petronia. There was no traffic, not that it would slow me down. I weaved my way through the trashed streets, getting off my bike when the road got too bad. There was a lane cleared in the middle of Southard, on which I again was going the wrong way. Another National Guard vehicle roared toward me, and I pulled to the side of the road. After it had stormed past, I continued on my way, teeth clenched.

I wanted Frank to myself.

And Jade.

44

LENNY WAS RIGHT, FIVE BROTHERS WAS OPEN, but I coasted past and turned left onto Grinnell. The road was fairly clear of large debris but covered in leaves from stripped trees. There were multiple lanes that fed from Grinnell between Southard and Fleming. I rode slowly and watched ahead for a large white house. The one on the corner between Southard and Lowe was large and white but boarded up tight.

Past Lowe the houses were yellow, faint blue, and all two-story on the right side. Cornish Lane was next on the left side, and all the homes were single-story, but a large white two-story with double porches was just past Cornish, and it was occupied. Some of the shutters were off and windows were open. I rode up the sidewalk on the other side of the street and glanced to my left as I passed. The house had a driveway, and sitting in it was a large jacked-up black Ford truck with oversize tires. The bed was covered over with an armored plastic lid—Tonneau cover, they call them. A yellow kayak was strapped to the roof of the truck.

I pedaled on, but my treasure hunter's intuition was redlined. Next was Hibiscus Lane—didn't Bruiser mention that his friend on Hibiscus said Jade bought a house around the corner? My gut said to return to the big white house between Cornish and Hibiscus.

I climbed off my bike, crossed the road, and walked it back down the sidewalk. At Hibiscus, just before the big white house, was a deserted, run-down one-story house. I laid my bike in the bushes there and walked down Hibiscus to see if I could glimpse the white house from behind.

WHOOSH! The roar of a private jet descending toward the airport tore at the sky overhead. Probably a VIP politician visitor grandstanding for a television crew or a wealthy resident who'd paid someone to get access back to the island. No way that small jet was full of relief supplies.

White paint hung in peels off every wall on the big house. The backyard was overgrown with weeds. The house had great bones but needed a complete restoration, a pool, and landscaping to realize its full potential.

I heard a door open.

"I won't be long," a male voice said. I cringed. It was Frank.

Slam. The sound echoed through the otherwise vacant neighborhood. I bent down and hurried forward between the one-story house and its scrubby landscaping on the side of Hibiscus Lane. As I reached the front I peered around the corner.

Frank walked down the steps at the end of the porch. He hesitated and glanced to the left up toward Hibiscus—if he turned that way I'd have to dive into the shrubs. But he turned to the right and walked down Grinnell. I moved slowly up the edge of the yard and saw him disappear around the corner at Southard.

Screw it.

I stepped out onto the sidewalk and walked quickly to the gate next to the driveway, up the steps, and across the wood porch. The entry door was on the side. Should I knock? Call out her name?

No.

I turned the handle and pushed the door open.

"You forget your money?" Jade called out from a room straight ahead and to the right.

When I walked in, her mouth fell open and her eyes bugged wide.

"What are you doing—" She stopped short. "Thank God you're here! Frank captured me—he's holding me hostage."

There were two glasses with ice on the counter next to a bottle of Pilar dark rum and a container of fruit juice.

"Bullshit, Jade."

Her face turned serious. "What do you mean?"

"Is Frank forcing you to drink rum punch?"

She crossed her arms. There was a knife on the counter next to a lime. She eyed it quickly.

"What the hell are you doing, Jade?"

"That money's half mine. I searched my entire life—"

"What about Greg Holmes, the man Frank murdered? You willing to take half the credit for that, too? Or don't you care how he got the money?"

She stepped closer to where the knife was on the counter.

"Frank's crazy! I had nothing to do with that."

"Other than tricking me to risk my life flying him out there only to double-cross me twice, you mean? You two were in on this together the whole time. You lied to me, used me—"

"I saved you from drowning in that tunnel, Buck. That would have been the easiest solution but I—"

"Spare me. At first I couldn't figure it out until I realized you weren't done using me yet. You wanted me to find the other half of the tunnel, didn't you?" My shout caused her to shout back.

"My father left me that map—it's my legacy!"

"It's government money, Jade. If you calm down I'll tell you about it."

"What are you talking about? My father—*our* fathers—left it there!"

"That's right, they did. They were government agents."

"Ha! That's—what—are you crazy? Your old man, maybe—that would explain things—"

"Yours too, Jade."

"What kind of crap are you talking? How many times have we discussed their pasts over the past couple weeks? And the dope we found in the tunnels? And my father getting killed."

I stepped closer to her. "He didn't, Jade. I met him last night, in Bogotá. He's a DEA agent—"

"Bogotá? You were here—we had a hurricane, remember?"

"One of the numbers in my father's notebook was to the U.S. Embassy in Bogotá. I called it and a man answered—a DEA agent—so I flew there yesterday. It took all day. Long story short—"

"Long story, short on truth—"

"I met him, Jade. He was the man in the picture." I pulled the photo out of my shirt pocket. "He's all silver now—"

The floor creaked behind me—

I spun—*CRACK!* A heavy weight landed on my shoulder, just missing my head. Pain shot through my left collarbone.

Frank was there, the .357 Magnum that he'd just hit me with in one hand, a tray with two *café con leches* in the other.

"What are you doing here, Reilly?"

I kicked the tray, and coffee exploded over his chest.

"Aagghh!"

I lunged for the gun, but he punched my kidney with his left hand, doubling me over.

A sudden weight was on my back, an arm around my neck. Jade swung the knife from the counter in front of my face, but I spun around and flung her to the floor near Frank.

"Enough!" he said.

He stood with the Magnum pointed at my chest.

No doubt in my mind he'd shoot.

45

THE ROPES FRANK USED TO TIE ME TO THE CHAIR cut into my wrists.

"There's National Guard all over this island," I said.

"Here to clean the roads so we can get out of here," Frank said.

I turned to Jade. She'd carried a suitcase down from upstairs. Her eyes wouldn't meet mine.

"He's alive, Jade. He knows he screwed up—"

"Stop it!" she said.

"He couldn't come back—"

"What's he talking about?" Frank said.

"Nothing—lies!"

"Tommy Diaz is alive, Frank."

I might have said Mars was made of fish dip, given his expression.

"That's funny, Reilly."

"I met him yesterday—"

"Buck claims he flew to Bogotá yesterday."

"I knew you flew out," Frank said. "Thought you'd got smart and ran."

I shook my head. "I followed up on information in my father's papers. The ones I found in the second tunnel. Jade took the cocaine, I took the notebooks—"

"Cocaine?" His head swiveled in slow motion to face her.

"It was crap. I dumped it."

"Tommy was—*is*—DEA," I said.

Frank's head robotically swiveled back.

"You were their cutout, Frank, back in the day. You and your team of muscle gave them legitimacy. But all the drugs were burned as soon as you delivered them."

"You're full of shit. Tommy was murdered. Crazy Charlie—your old man went for vengeance—"

"Nope. He was deep undercover, too. Both of them were. Tommy told me the whole story."

Jade and Frank exchanged a glance.

"Is he full of shit or what?" Jade said. "DEA? No way—he would've come back for me."

"He couldn't, Jade, without putting you at risk—"

"At risk?" She kicked her suitcase over.

Frank now had a big smile on his face. "This is great," he said. "I don't have to feel guilty anymore. D-E-fuckin'-A?"

Jade crossed her arms. "Guilty for what?"

"Tommy and Charlie were screwing me. I knew it. They never intended to pay me, and when things started to go to shit for Escobar, your old men got all buddy-buddy with the Cali cartel. I love it!"

"Love what, Frank?" I said.

"My conscience is clear, that's what." His smile grew wider. "I told Escobar's people that Tommy and Charlie were double-timing them with Cali."

"You *what?*" Jade said.

"All this time, I thought that got Tommy killed—Charlie, too, when he disappeared. It worked, though. The business fell right into my lap—"

"And you got busted the minute you tried to do something on your own, you dumb-ass," Jade said. "You ratted my father out!"

"Damn straight. They hadn't paid me squat. DEA? No shit, ha!"

She launched herself at him, fists flying. Frank's gun toppled to the floor. Jade clung to his shoulders, kicking hard and wailing like a feral cat on the attack. Frank windmilled his arms, trying to swat her.

I swung my weight to the side, and the chair toppled toward Frank's gun. The gun was right by my face.

"How could you do that?" Jade kept doing all the damage she could. "My father! You were friends!"

A roar emanated from deep inside Frank. He dropped a knee, and Jade fell to the side. He grabbed her by the waist and flung her over his head.

It could hardly have been worse. Her head hit the edge of the coffee table, and she ended up flat on her back on the wood floor.

Motionless.

I struggled against the ropes—the gun so close. Frank saw it, too.

"You son of a bitch."

Like a place kicker, he stepped forward to plant his front foot and lift his back one. Then all I saw was his boot coming forward—

WHAP!

46

"BUCK! CAN YOU HEAR ME?" my mother called out from the barn. My brother and I were fishing. We stood on the water.

"We're in trouble," Ben said.

"Buck!"

The images of our pond, the barn in the distance, my mother calling all faded away.

"He's coming to."

Above me was a red-haired angel with concern etched across her face.

"Scarlet! Where's Ben?"

"Ben who?"

Pain rocked my head as I sat forward, a pool of blood on the floor. I felt my face—sharp pain, blood. I felt my nose—

"It's broken, Buck."

"Not for the first time," I said.

"The hell happened?" Lenny said. "Frank fuck your face up?"

My tunnel vision expanded and there were Lenny Jackson, Truck, and Bruiser Lewis hovering over me. Ray peered around from behind Scarlet.

"You look like hell," he said.

I saw the boot coming at me—the kickoff.

Frank.

"Jade? Did Frank kill her?"

"On the couch," Truck said. "Got ice on her head. Hell of a knot there."

I managed to get up on my knees—stars flashed behind my eyes—and crawl to the couch. Jade was stretched out face up, tracks of tears down her temples.

"You okay?" I said.

She didn't look at me. "Why wouldn't he have come back?"

"Those were bloody times, Jade." My voice was low. "Escobar's people killed thousands, entire families they considered traitors." I paused. "Frank ratting him out forced him into deep hiding. Tommy told me the cartel would have killed his entire family—you, Jade."

She turned to face me. "Nearly thirty years have passed."

I nodded. What could be said? I considered Diaz a piece of shit for the same reason. I couldn't tell her that, though. I'd have to think of something.

"Excuse me, you guys," Truck said, "but where's Frank Graves?"

I glanced up. How much time had passed? There was blood on the floor near the broken chair, still wet. Couldn't have been long.

"Is there a jacked-up black Ford 250 in the driveway?" I said.

"Driveway's empty," Ray said.

"He's bolted."

"With the money?" Lenny said.

"And my truck." Jade sat up. "That son of a bitch is the reason I have no family."

Scarlet's forehead wrinkled. "Can someone explain what's going on?"

I stood up, the pain in my face so sharp I winced. "Frank's the guy who kidnapped me and made me fly him out to Woman Key in the storm." I glanced at Jade. "He killed Greg Holmes out there."

"Caretaker at Ballast Key?" Ray said.

I nodded.

"Roads are still closed up the Keys," Bruiser said.

"Need to get the word out," Truck said.

"We have the radio at the airport," Ray said.

"I have my sat-phone." Scarlet pulled the phone out of her back pocket.

"Ain't no phones working," Bruiser said. "Who you gonna call?"

Scarlet smiled. "Red Cross to the rescue."

Truck and Bruiser shared a she's-crazy glance.

"They can rouse the National Guard troops here," she said.

"Perfect!" I said.

"Tell them he stole my truck," Jade said.

Scarlet nodded. Within a moment she was on the phone with her Red Cross colleagues. She explained there had been a robbery and a man had fled in a black Ford F-250—

"There's a black Tonneau cover on the back," Jade said. She glanced at me. "And a Thompson submachine gun inside."

Scarlet's eyes widened.

"Say he's armed and to just hold his truck wherever they find it," I said. "Like it's a routine traffic stop due to the storm."

Scarlet relayed the information.

"How'd you all get here?" I said.

"I walked," Scarlet said.

"We got bikes," Truck said. Ray, Lenny, and Bruiser nodded.

From behind the larger-than-life Lewis brothers came a determined voice.

"Let's get him."

The men stepped aside. Jade stood there, her eyes dark.

"Let's hope Scarlet's Red Cross contacts can—"

BRING-BRING.

BRING-BRING.

It was the first mechanical sound any of us had heard since Irma killed power for hundreds of miles. It was Scarlet's satellite phone.

"Hello?" Scarlet's eyes opened wide. "Great, where?"

She put the phone on "speaker."

"The truck's stopped at the corner of Pearl and Roosevelt in the Meadows," the man said. "Funny thing is, the National Guard's there with a backhoe cleaning up the road, so it really *is* just a storm-related delay—"

"Just keep him there," I said.

"Let's go!" Jade said.

"Wait!" Scarlet said. "How are we going to get there?"

"You're staying here—this guy's dangerous!" I grabbed Ray by the shoulder. "You stay with Scarlet. This isn't your fight. These guys can help us. Jade, you should—"

"Let's go. Now!" she said.

Lenny, Truck, and Bruiser were out the door. They'd laid their bikes down in the driveway. Mine was in the neighbor's yard.

Jade pulled her bike from the side of the house and we set out down Grinnell like we were in the Tour de France. We turned up the wrong way on Southard and pedaled our asses off toward White Street.

"Who's that redhead?" Jade had pulled up next to me. "Ex-girlfriend?"

I glanced at her out of the corner of my eye. "A lot more than that."

"The hell we gonna do when we get to Frank?" Lenny said. "Dude has a machine gun."

"Kick some ass," Bruiser said. He pulled his shirt up to show a handgun wedged in his belt.

"We'll figure it out when we get there," I said. "Don't shoot him. though. Not worth going to jail for."

Truck laughed. "You think too much, Reilly. He'd kill all of us to get away. Don't cut him any slack."

Greg had pointed to me and asked why I shot him just before he died. I cringed.

Paybacks are hell.

47

WE SPLIT UP AT OLIVIA AND FLORIDA STREETS, a block from where Frank had been stopped. Truck and Bruiser came with me down Olivia and we stopped at Pearl. Roosevelt was to our right. Lenny and Jade had gone down Florida and were supposed to stop at Roosevelt and keep an eye out in case Frank turned back toward downtown.

"There's a jacked-up black Ford F-250 over there," Bruiser said.

The sound of heavy equipment at work to clear Roosevelt, the main road in and out of downtown Key West, gave me hope that Frank couldn't escape to the left toward the one-way off the island. A Humvee was parked on Roosevelt, blocking access to the left. Pearl dead-ended onto Roosevelt, and Bayview Park was beyond that. There were a couple of men dressed in tan camouflage military fatigues in the intersection with guns slung on their backs watching the roadwork. Straight ahead was Bayview Park.

"You guys ride side by side and I'll stay tight behind you so Frank can't see me," I said.

Truck and Bruiser pulled out like a pair of battle tanks. I followed.

We kept a casual pace and closed in on the Ford, now a half block away. The odds were finally in my favor. Frank had got the best of me at every turn, but this would be different.

Movement caught my attention off to the right—a bicycle was speeding down Roosevelt toward the intersection. A man—Lenny—was pedaling hard behind it.

"Stop!" A National Guardsman shouted.

Jade was on the lead bike, headed straight for the Ford. What the hell was she—

"Faster!" I yelled to the brothers ahead of me.

They were too slow to accelerate—Jade closed fast. I veered to the left around Bruiser and sped ahead to reach the driver's side of the Ford just as Jade arrived at the passenger side.

"Help! Please help me!" Jade's loud pleas attracted the attention of the National Guardsmen and the road crew. She waved wildly to them.

From the Ford' side mirror, I saw Frank's face twist with rage at the sight of Jade, who continued to yell.

"This is my truck—this man stole it!"

I jumped off my bike—

Bruiser flew by Jade on the right side of the Ford and turned in front of it.

I lunged for the driver's side handle, but Frank hit the gas and the Ford shot forward just as Bruiser pulled in front of it. The Ford hit him and launched him into the air. He fell into a groaning heap.

"Goddamn!" Lenny said.

Jade was in the middle of Roosevelt, and Frank had to know he'd be trapped if he turned back toward downtown. He sped up, cut past the Humvee that blocked Roosevelt to the left, swerved around Jade, and jumped the curb into Bayview Park. He veered around trees, swerved in a circle, and cut past the Veterans Memorial Garden.

The National Guardsmen stood frozen with their mouths wide open. Jade had already lit out after Frank on foot. Did she *want* him to run over her? Lenny and I took off on our bikes. Truck jumped off his bike to check Bruiser, who sat in the road, cursing.

I was gaining on Frank. He swerved around the circular Veterans Memorial and sideswiped a palm tree.

Jade had raced across the open field and thrown her bike down on Virginia Street in front of where Frank had no choice but to exit due to the sports courts, Veterans Memorial, and other structures. He glanced quickly in all directions.

I was starting to close in on him, bent over my bike, when he fired his damn Magnum at me! And then I saw the Ford suddenly accelerate toward Jade.

She back-stepped to the far side of Virginia Street, staring aghast as Frank sped toward her. He was going to kill her.

Suddenly a pink blur slashed in from the right—down Virginia Street—

KABOOM!

The pink rocket—it was a van from the Five-6's taxi company—sped in front of Frank's truck at high speed and intercepted the Ford before it could hit Jade.

She stood frozen with her back against a fence and her arms across her chest. The sudden impact had caused Frank to smash his head on the windshield—hard. The safety glass was cracked and bloody.

Frank was slumped over the wheel, blood trickling out of his mouth and off his forehead. I pulled open the driver's-side door, grabbed his pistol off the floor, and threw it deep into the bushes.

I ran around to the passenger side of the pink van just as the side door slid wide.

Scarlet and Ray Floyd tumbled out onto the road.

"Holy crap, that dude's crazy!" Ray said.

Scarlet looked back over her shoulder. "He's unconscious, Buck—hurt bad."

The driver had intentionally pulled the van into the path of the Ford—and Frank had plowed directly into the driver's side. Now the driver's door was collapsed in on the man behind the wheel.

I rushed to check on the driver. He had on a silver business suit—

Oh no.

The blood on the man's suit had dripped from his mouth down across the fine silver sheen of his close-cropped beard.

"That taxi saved my life," Jade said.

She tried to climb inside the van—I blocked her.

"Is he okay?" she said. "He saved my life!"

"Wait here," I said.

Back inside, I put my fingers on the man's neck.

Tommy Diaz was not okay.

"Is he dead?" Jade said.

"I'm afraid so."

She squirmed around to look at Ray and Scarlet. "Who was he? Why did he do that?"

"Jade—"

"He had to see the Ford coming—why would he do that?"

Tears formed in Jade's eyes. She looked from me to the once-handsome man now crumpled into the dash.

The private jet I'd seen earlier. It wasn't a VIP politician, at least not one coming for a photo op. It had been a relief worker, but for a different disaster.

"It's Tommy Diaz," I said.

Tears burst from her eyes.

I held her as she cried and looked past me to the silver-haired man who'd returned to save his daughter.

"My daddy saved my life! He gave his life to save mine!"

48

WE SAT ON JADE'S FRONT PORCH. The air was still, humid, and smelled of mold and putrefaction. Water bottles and plastic cups of Pilar rum provided limited relief from the heat and the pain.

"We need some weed," Lenny said.

"Okay, Mr. Councilman," I said.

"You right," said Bruiser, his left arm in a homemade sling. "Freaking arm's busted, man."

Truck poured more rum into Bruiser's cup. "This doctor says more rum, less whine."

Jade was in the kitchen salvaging whatever food hadn't spoiled in the days since Irma had killed the electricity.

We'd all slept on Jade's floor last night. Still numb, we'd hung out in her neighborhood all morning, helped to pick up the road, and stuck close to her. Jade and I shared a unique, bizarre connection that would be inexplicable to anyone but us. I wasn't sure I could ever trust her, but I understood her. And that was enough.

The noonday sun was high in the sky, but the covered porch provided shade. Once we'd proved to the National Guardsmen that the Ford belonged to Jade, she was allowed to take it. Nobody had asked to check under the Tonneau cover.

Frank Graves had been arrested and charged with vehicular manslaughter for killing Tommy Diaz. Frank would claim that Tommy had pulled in front of him, but I had every intention of telling the police about Greg Holmes, too. For now, Jade's well-being was a more immediate concern.

Scarlet told us that Tommy had appeared in a taxi and, when Ray filled him in on the situation, flashed his DEA credentials to the driver and commandeered the vehicle. Ray told him where to go. They saw the Ford swerve wildly across the open field in Bayview Park before it zeroed in on Jade.

We had finished off the rum and were now all standing in her driveway by her truck, with its crunched front end and broken windshield. Jade handed me the keys, and I unlocked the Tonneau cover over the bed. Other than Jade, only one of them had any idea what was there, so a sense of expectation was thick in the muggy air.

I pressed the button and lifted the lid, which screeched. Eight L.L. Bean duffel bags were piled neatly inside next to—

"Is that a Thompson submachine gun?" Ray said.

"I'm guessing it ain't Frank's luggage," Truck said.

I pulled a bag forward and unzipped it. The high-noon sun illuminated the contents packed tight inside.

"Godamighty," Bruiser said.

"King Buck rides again." Scarlet's voice was a whisper.

"This is drug money," I said.

Jade frowned. She walked back onto the porch and sat in one of the chairs.

I closed the lid and relocked it, and we followed after her.

"Cops know about that shit?" Truck said.

I put my hands on my hips. "Technically—"

"It's government money, *technically*," Jade said.

"Damn." Lenny said. "I could run for mayor with that kind of stash—the state Senate!"

"We could repair Betty," Ray said.

Jade got up and walked inside, and I followed.

She was in the kitchen, facing out a window to stare across the overgrown backyard. I stood behind her. She didn't turn around.

"That's my—*our*—money, Buck."

"Our fathers were cops, not smugglers."

"I don't care. I want half. Four bags for you, four for me."

"And I want you to have it, but—" I put my hand on her shoulder. She shrugged it off and spun around to face me. "Let's think about it," I said.

"Screw you. I've thought about it my whole life."

The image of silver-haired Tommy in the back of the Mercedes in Bogotá flashed forward to him dead behind the wheel of the Five-6's taxi. She must have read my expression—she pressed her eyes closed and tears seeped out between her pinched lids.

"I'm sorry," I said. I wrapped my arms around her.

She shook in my arms, whuffled and—

"Goddamn it all!" She pushed me back a step.

Scarlet was peering in the window at us.

49

I DROVE THE FORD. JADE SAT IN THE MIDDLE, and Lenny was on the passenger side. The truck's front end was badly damaged, but the vehicle was drivable. Emergency workers were thick on the highway north. Once past Sugarloaf Key, trees, trash, residential debris, and boats far from the water lined the highway in tall piles.

We used Lenny's credentials to get up past the roadblocks. After we crossed the trash-covered bridge onto Cudjoe Key, where Irma's eye had hit, the scene looked like a carpet-bombed Baghdad.

Every home we passed was heavily damaged. Fallen trees had cut several in half, and others were windowless, roofless concrete shells. Trailers had been tossed about like Legos, and there were more boats shoved to the sides of the highway than I'd ever seen in a marina.

The scene continued on Big Torch Key, Summerland, Ramrod, and Big Pine. As we drove slowly up A1A, piles of refuse were two stories high on both sides of the highway. Jade stared straight ahead as we passed by Bahia Honda State Park—its leaves and foliage wiped from green to brown—and onward to the Seven Mile Bridge.

"Where are we going?" she said.

The view from the bridge was milky-green water dotted with flotsam as far as the eye could see. Rogue boats floated aimlessly, and several were half-sunk.

"Marathon High School on Sombrero Road was the closest refuge of last resort," Lenny said. "I want to check on them."

Long-faced men and woman stood on the sidewalks of Sombrero Road staring at us as if in a fog. The school was a three-story concrete structure that had the look of a military armory.

"Good choice for a shelter," I said.

People milled around the parking lot like the refuges they were—Irma refugees still here because they'd lost everything. I parked in the far end of the lot near the road. Dozens of people filled the lot. There was nowhere for them to go.

"This is the saddest thing I've ever seen," Jade said.

Lenny popped the door open. "I'm going to find the administrator."

Near the truck was a little girl leaning against her father's leg and clutching a soiled teddy bear. She stared up at us. Her face was brown with dirt, her eyes blank. Her father was in no better shape.

"Where's her mother?" Jade whispered.

Lenny walked back to the truck with a man who looked like he hadn't slept in days. People spoke to him as they passed by.

"Mind if I stand on your bent-up hood?" Lenny said when they reached the truck. "Want to let these people know the Key West City Council will help any way we can."

He struggled to climb onto the front bumper but finally pulled himself up to the Ford's hood. He raised his hands and beckoned people to come closer. Some listened while others stared glassy-eyed or seemed to ignore him entirely. The little girl with the teddy bear looked up.

"You people been through hell," Lenny said, "but you're alive."

The administrator glanced inside the truck. I suspected he was half the age he looked.

"Do not give up hope!" Lenny raised his arms.

"Hope's not going to feed those hungry kids," Jade said.

"And they probably didn't have insurance," I said. "They won't get anything back."

Lenny continued giving it his best effort to instill hope into the hopeless.

"Let's get out," I said. Jade nodded even though the air conditioning was on. I killed the ignition.

We got out of the truck and I walked to the back with the keys in my hand.

"We could help save their lives," I said.

Jade rolled her eyes. But then she saw the little girl with the teddy bear watching us.

Jade pursed her lips. "I'm good for one bag, but that's it."

I pushed the button and the Tonneau cover opened. The screech interrupted Lenny. He glanced back and then turned around, facing us.

"Buck? What the hell are you doing?"

I waved a couple of fingers, summoning him. "What do you think?"

"One bag," Jade said, her eyes sparkling.

Lenny jogged to the back of the truck, the administrator in tow. He beckoned the officers from the sheriff's department near the entrance to the school-cum-shelter.

"The hell, man? You some seriously crazy mofos," Lenny said, smiling and talking at the same time. "Everybody gather round here!" he shouted. "We got something for you."

"No names, Lenny," I said.

About fifty people gathered around the truck.

"Make room for that little girl ... and her father." Jade's voice cracked as she pointed to teddy-bear girl in the back. "Get her up front."

I hid the Thompson under a few bags in the back of the bed.

"Make a line, people!"

They fell into line. Lenny was a take-charge kind of guy.

I handed Jade a bound stack of $5,000 bills in each hand. She hesitated, then bent down and handed the money to the little girl's father.

Word traveled fast through the crowd. The policemen's eyes bulged, and they jumped to attention and stood either side of the bumper.

"On behalf of the people of Key West—" Lenny said.

"And the U.S. government—" I said.

"And, ah, these good citizens here—" Lenny's voice cracked, and tears trickled down his face.

Some recipients were so shell-shocked we might have been handing them water bottles. Others hooted and jumped up and down. Still others hollered out things like "God bless you!" and "God bless America!"

I could hardly breathe from being choked up.

Jade alternated between the occasional tear and laughing as she reached down and handed out what amounted to tens and then hundreds of thousands of dollars.

And ultimately over a million.

EPILOGUE

One Month Later

THE SUN WAS BRIGHT ON THE AFTERDECK OF LOUIE'S BACKYARD. Scarlet and I sat at the rail on the corner overlooking Dog Beach and the milky sea at low tide. Exposed sand, normally underwater, extended the length of the patio. A black Lab puppy chased a tennis ball into the shallows.

Scarlet's copper hair glistened against the green water backdrop. Her white sundress revealed tanned, freckled shoulders along with her defined triceps. She was in amazing condition. Motherhood had agreed with her.

My eyes followed the black Lab back to the handsome young boy who kept throwing the ball into the surf, to the puppy's delight. The boy was tall, had sandy blond shoulder-length hair, and sharp blue eyes.

"Another Mojito?" the waiter said.

"Yes, please," I said.

Scarlet shook her head. "No, thanks."

The black Lab gave a happy bark, and the boy threw the ball deeper into the water. The puppy splashed fearlessly into the waves.

"Why Winter Park?" I said.

"My mother's there. She helps out. Good schools, too."

She followed my stare to the boy and his puppy, then drained the remains of her Mojito.

"Why Key West?" she said.

I nodded toward the water. "Last Resort Charter and Salvage."

"Last Resort. Catchy." Her mouth twisted.

"Double meaning. Back in the seventies, Key West was known as the last resort—southernmost point and all."

"And the other meaning?"

I laughed. "Is that a rhetorical question?"

Scarlet stared into the mint-covered ice of her glass. She sat up straight. "So what's the story with Jade? Are you two together?"

The puppy barked. The boy ran up the beach.

"Not romantic. Never was. We're like siblings. Our fathers' past histories brought us together, intertwined in ways that had to be dealt with. Hard to explain."

"I heard about her giving that money away. You gave some of yours?"

"Most." I grinned.

Scarlet's eyes grew wide for a moment, and a smirk bent the corners of her lips. "You certainly have changed. King Buck would have never given away a million dollars."

My lips pressed tight. The new drink arrived and I took a sip.

The boy and the dog disappeared past the wooden fence of the property beyond Dog Beach. I craned my head over the rail and saw they were already running back up the beach toward us. The boy's laugh made me smile.

"He's not the only one who loves that puppy," Scarlet said. "It was a wonderful gift—I'm sorry if I seemed reluctant at the time."

"He was an orphan. His family was killed…in the storm."

Did Scarlet hear my voice crack? I took a long pull on the cocktail. It was syrupy sweet. She reached out and touched my cheek, just for a moment.

"So what happened with Craig?"

She pulled her hand away. "Once he knew the truth about our son, there was no way he was staying." Her focus shifted toward the horizon. "He refused to live a lie."

"But you did," I said.

Her gaze remained out to sea. Who was I to judge Scarlet? After all I'd done to her? And after all she'd done for me?

"You'd made your choice." She turned to face me. Her green eyes were clear and unblinking. "Then so much time had gone by."

"Ten years, to be exact."

"Ten years and two months." Her eyes smiled even if her lips were taut.

My throat constricted, my cheeks felt warm, and my eyes brimmed.

"Are you ready to meet Charlie?" she said.

The dam broke and tears tore down my cheeks. She wiped them away with her thumbs. A shudder passed through me.

"Yes, I am."

THE END

Acknowledgements

I first learned of the existence of underground tunnels in Key West from my friend and fishing guide, Pepe Gonzalez of Pepe's Charters while we were hunting for tarpon several summers ago. Prohibition era booze smugglers used the tunnels, and while not widely known about, they do exist. Thanks, Pepe.

When I first lived in the Keys in the 1970's and 1980's it was like the wild, wild west, to say the least. Prohibition had long ago been repealed, but marijuana and later cocaine smuggling had become the modern reincarnation. Crazed Colombians, Bolivians, Peruvians and others provided the supply, and there was no shortage of demand. When law enforcement finally caught up, the streets of South Florida had already been permeated with blood.

Pablo Escobar had been the head of the Medellín Cartel, the first major criminal organization to successfully smuggle vast amounts of illegal drugs into urban and often remote areas of the United States, and the islands around Key West had been a popular drop zone. Escobar was one of the most vicious terrorists of our time, killing over 1,000 policemen in Medellín alone, and he even blew up a commercial Avianca flight full of regular people targeting one Colombian politician who opposed him. Escobar's reign of terror was facilitated by corrupt law enforcement and politicians until a vigilante group called *Perseguidos por Pablo Escobar*, which translates to People Persecuted by Pablo Escobar, or Los Pepes, was formed by Colombian paramilitary leaders, citizens, competing drug lords and frustrated officials. Los Pepes was and aided by the CIA, DEA and they fought violence with violence.

The methodologies of Los Pepes were no less brutal than those of the Medellín Cartel, but they succeeded in eliminating many cartel members, along with their sympathizers, government enablers, and finally on December 2, 1993, Carlos Escobar was killed. Los Pepes disbanded shortly thereafter. Exactly who all of the leaders or strategists of Los Pepes had been was never publically confirmed.

On September 10, 2017, Hurricane Irma made landfall in the Florida Keys after wreaking havoc through the Caribbean and Cuba. The damage to the Keys, as well as parts of Florida and the Caribbean was extensive. My friends Shawn Martin and Noel Calzolano rode out Irma from our house in Key West, and like others who had stayed behind, did what they could to help the subsequent clean-up around the island and up the Keys. Nearly all my old Conch friends from the Keys, most of who had never evacuated for a hurricane in their lives, said they'd never stay again after having survived Irma. Thank you to everyone who contributed to the cleanup, and our hearts still go out to the hundreds whose homes were flattened, their boats tossed about like toys and their lives forever altered. Keys Strong.

Thank you to my friend, Carl Grooms for his aviation guidance, professional photographer, Deborah Grooms for graciously taking my new author photo, Preston Brewer for having the Navy League of Key West help the Writers for Keys Hurricane Relief, a group of 20+ authors I co-founded with Wayne Stinnett to raise money for victims of Irma through Task Force Dagger and Star of the Sea, and singer songwriter, Keith Sykes, for co-writing Hanging Out at Le Select, a song we co-wrote and Keith recorded, the proceeds of which were used to also raise money for hurricane relief.

Thank you to Renni Browne, editor extraordinaire, and Ross Browne of The Editorial Department, who together with the TED team have edited every Buck Reilly novel; Tim Harkness for creating the book cover, the series logo and marketing materials; Ann-Marie Nieves of Get Red PR for her advice and for being my longtime publicist.

Thank you to the fans of the Buck Reilly series, for your patience, dedication and support. Hopefully, in the near future, my schedule will allow me to write more than one book a year, or so.

Special thanks to Ron and Linda Weiner, Holly, Bailey, Cortney and future son-in-law Will Prendergast for their love and support as I multi-task my way through life.

About the author

John H. Cunningham is the author of the best selling, seven book, Buck Reilly adventure series, which includes Red Right Return, Green to Go, Crystal Blue, Second Chance Gold, Maroon Rising, Free Fall to Black and Silver Goodbye. Through the years, John has been a bouncer at a Key West nightclub, a diver, pilot, magazine editor, commercial developer, song writer and global traveler. He has either lived in or visited the many island locations that populate the series, and has experienced or witnessed enough craziness and wild times to keep the Buck Reilly series flowing.

John mixes fact with fiction and often includes real people in his novels, like Jimmy Buffett, Chris Blackwell, Matt Hoggatt, Thom Shepherd, Dave McKenney, Keith Sykes, Marius Stakelborough, Bruno Magras and Bankie Banx to augment the reader's experience. Adhering to the old maxim, "write what you know," John's books have an authenticity and immediacy that have earned a loyal following and strong reviews. Buck Reilly is a reflection of us all, including our frailties, strengths, dreams, fears, successes, failures, mistakes and occasional victories. No government agency, team of soldiers, unlimited cash, or secret agents are coming to his rescue, because, well they're not coming to mine either. How about you?

John lives in Virginia and Key West, and spends much of his time traveling. His choices for the places and plots that populate the Buck Reilly series include many subjects that he loves: Key West, Cuba, Jamaica, and multiple Caribbean settings, along with amphibious aircraft, colorful characters, and stories that concern themselves with the same tensions and issues that affect all of our lives.

Book links:

RED RIGHT RETURN (Buck Reilly book 1): http://www.amazon.com/Right-Return-Reilly-Adventure-Series-ebook/dp/B00D8HOSN2/ref=pd_sim_kstore_2?ie=UTF8&refRID=0H9XXB0JPPWTQPP251FB

GREEN TO GO (Buck Reilly book 2): http://www.amazon.com/Green-Buck-Reilly-Adventure-Series-ebook/dp/B00D6Q0WOE/ref=pd_sim_kstore_1?ie=UTF8&refRID=1AH2GWXXGX0MV0N3RDM8

CRYSTAL BLUE (Buck Reilly book 3): http://www.amazon.com/Crystal-Blue-Reilly-Adventure-Series-ebook/dp/B00EWSAZ92/ref=pd_sim_kstore_2?ie=UTF8&refRID=14902YRMCYTEGSMTTYHQ

SECOND CHANCE GOLD (Buck Reilly book 4): http://www.amazon.com/Second-Chance-Reilly-Adventure-Series/dp/0985442271/ref=pd_sim_14_2?ie=UTF8&refRID=0CEEBYEWA7C7E50NGRGH

MAROON RISING (Buck Reilly book 5): https://www.amazon.com/Maroon-Rising-Buck-Reilly-Adventure-ebook/dp/B016QUC76C

FREE FALL TO BLACK (Buck Reilly book 6): https://www.amazon.com/Free-Fall-Black-Reilly-Adventure/dp/0998796506

Music links:

"THE BALLAD OF BUCK REILLY" (Download the song or all of Workaholic in Recovery from iTunes at): https://itunes.apple.com/us/album/workaholic-in-recovery/id908713680

"RUM PUNCH" by Thom Shepherd, and co-written by John H. Cunningham, is available on iTunes at: https://itunes.apple.com/us/album/rum-punch-single/id1051324975

"LONG VIEW OFF A SHORT PIER" by Dave McKenney and co-written by John H. Cunningham, is available on iTunes at: https://itunes.apple.com/us/album/back-in-time/id1161935367?ign-mpt=uo%3D4#

"HANGING OUT AT LE SELECT" by Keith Sykes and co-written by John H. Cunningham, is available on CD Baby at: https://store.cdbaby.com/cd/keithsykes1

CPSIA information can be obtained
at www.ICGtesting.com
Printed in the USA
LVHW112150280519
619376LV00001B/108/P